Best Wishes

16.5.18

Elizabeth Parker
LIZZIE´S PARADISE

Lizzie´s Paradise
© Text Elizabeth Parker 1997
© Illustrations Martina Selway 1997

Die Deutsche Bibliothek - CIP-Einheitsaufnahme:

Parker, Elizabeth:
Lizzie´s paradise / Elizabeth Parker. - Ratingen/Deutschland :
Melina-Verl., 1997
Dt. Ausg. u.d.T.: Parker, Elizabeth: Lizzie´s paradise
ISBN 3-929255-24-3

Publisher: Melina-Verlag
Am Weinhaus 6, D-40882 Ratingen/Germany
Telefon: 02102/9594-0, Telefax: 02102/9594-33
Internet: http://www. melina-verlag.de
Email: redaktion@melina-verlag.de
Lector: R.G. Chizlett
Cover and photos: Ewald Hein
Layout: Anette Hein
Print: MA-TISK, Slovenia

ISBN 3-929255-24-3

Elizabeth Parker

Lizzie´s Paradise

Illustrated by Martina Selway

Melina-Verlag

CONTENTS

To Alison, Arthur and Jim who made it possible!
Also to Judy Watson who patiently typed the manuscript so
that Ewald Hein, our Publisher could eventually read it and
believe in the book´s merit
To Ewald Hein "Vielen Dank".
L.P.

To my husband John Aston, who stayed at home.
M.S.

Lizzie´s Yacht Club is now under new ownership and is doing
well after many changes.

Shade from the midday sun

CHAPTER ONE

APHRODITE

But I, being poor, have only my dreams;

I have spread my dreams under your feet;

Tread softly, because you tread on my dreams.

W.B. Yeats

I went to Greece for the first time twenty-five years ago on a package tour with my second husband, Richard. We flew from Gatwick to Athens Airport, then took the small Olympic internal plane to Lesvos. The plane circled over the island, set in a turquoise sea, and then landed on a bumpy runway - trembling and shuddering until it stopped at a shed.

It was mid June and as we walked to the awaiting taxi I felt the sun's heat seeping into my skin and filling my body with energy. The sky was cloudless and a vivid blue and the air smelt fresh. The taxi took us on a circuitous route, up and over a barren mountain, then down through valleys where silvery green olives covered the land, their trunks gnarled and twisted into shapes resembling old people; there were large expanses of vines neatly aligned and producing fresh shoots; plantations of orange and lemon trees with leaves of vivid green shaded the wild flowers. The taxi slowed down to allow herds of goats and sheep to cross the road, they wore bells around their necks so the shepherd knew if they were to stray, the young goats scampered up the hillside, followed by the more sedate ewes who were heavy with milk.

Then we saw the translucent sea again. We had booked a small hotel "The Aphrodite" which our travel agent had described as "being basic, but in traditional Greek style, and right beside the sea". I had insisted on this last factor because I wanted to swim every morning, afternoon and evening. We were in a tiny village where white stone houses straggled up the hill from a small perfectly shaped, semi-circular bay. There was a protective harbour wall which sheltered several *caiques* painted in blues, greens and yellows. Our hotel was beside the shore at the end of the Mole. Richard paid the smiling taxi driver and with our suitcases we climbed the

10

steep, white stone steps between cascading red and white geraniums which were planted in containers of assorted colours and walked under an arch of purple Bougainvillaea to the open front door.

"*Elate*, come in and welcome", a silver-haired woman, dressed in black, appeared from the desk in the hall.

"Mr. and Mrs. Parker from England? How was your journey?" she spoke English with an American accent, "I am Eleni, please let me show you to your room, you must be tired."

We followed her up a flight of wooden stairs to a landing, then she opened the door to a darkened room, proudly stating - "This is our de-luxe suite". I couldn't actually see anything until she opened the shutters onto a balcony, and then focused on the lay-out of the room. There were two single, metal framed beds covered with white bedspreads, a coat stand stood in the corner, with a white chest of drawers beside it: two hard-backed cane chairs were placed beside the beds, and the floor was covered with linoleum with a striped cotton rug in between the beds: But it was the wallpaper that transfixed me - it was a faded red with sprigs of flowers which were patterned in horizontal lines, but the decorator had either been drunk or blind because the patterns did not align, this gave the room the impression of being askew, I wondered what Laura Ashley would have thought? There was one light bulb hanging in the centre of the room, with no shade; three pictures (photographs from a Swiss calender), showing snow covered scenery were in uneven symmetry on one wall and above our bed hung a plaster plaque of a parrot on a perch, but it was hanging up side down!

"Please to show you the shower."

Open mouthed we followed her to a sliding wooden door, she switched on the light to reveal a cupboard-like room with walls clad in plastic Fablon. Fitted into the corner was a wash basin which tilted from the wall at such an angle that you were guaranteed to overflow the bowl should you completely fill it up. There was a plastic shower hose attached to the wall, with a hole in the floor for the waste; Also, a lavatory which you could just get to if you closed the door. A large notice was selotaped to the wall: DO NOT PUT YOUR PAPER IN THE TOILET. IT IS DANGEROUS. PLEASE USE BIN PROVIDED. I thought the whole room was dangerous, noticing that the light switch was inside the shower room which bare wires exposed!

"Anything you need please tell me", Eleni said, "my brother knows all about mending, although he is a fisherman."

With that perplexing statement she left us alone.

"I can´t believe it", Richard angrily muttered, "I´m going to complain to the travel agent."

"Darling, it did say "Basic" and as we have never been to Greece before how do we know if any other hotel is different. But I love it! It´s so terrible it´s funny. Come and look at the view, we can sit outside and watch the sunset. The room is only for sleeping in."

We spent leisurely days wandering round the village, sipping strong coffee in the local *Kafenion*, ordering small plates of olives, cheese and bread to accompany our *ouzo*s (the aniseed flavoured drink so beloved of the Greeks). In the evenings we tasted the delicious home-made dishes of stuffed tomatoes or peppers, beans in a tomato and dill sauce and discovered the very strong garlic dish, Skorthalia, made of potato, oil, lemon and lashings of garlic, which traditionally was eaten with, beetroot, courgettes and cod. There was little choice because the village was isolated and they used the vegetables and produce that was in season and available.

We became acquainted with the local people. The women

who tirelessly washed down their front porches every morning, swept the steps and hung their blankets outside on the balcony to air. They then sat peeling the vegetables and preparing food for their families. They would take the prepared dishes to the local oven, which was shared by all villagers, returning later with the steaming platters to their own simple houses. There they would sit at a wooden table covered with a paper cloth, outside in the shade of a mulberry tree. Meals started with the local wine being served in squat thick tumblers and was always preceded with the toast - "*Yeia mas* - to us - here's health". Then everyone seated at the table would clink each other's glasses before supping the rough resinated liquor.

We enjoyed our conversations with Eleni's brother, Jannis, the fisherman. His face was deeply bronzed and lined by constant exposure to the wind and the salt spray. He sat patiently mending his nets each day after returning from his early morning catch. There was no engine on the *caique*, but he stood in the boat, using the rough hewn oars to glide through the calm sea to the spot where he knew the fishes swam. At dusk he would row out with his three pronged Kamaki and light the large kerosene lamp to attract an octopus, sometimes not returning until five a.m.

At night we would sit and watch the huge orange sun slowly sinking below the horizon, streaking the sky with yellow, purple and indigo, and with the sunset a silence would descend, when the cicadas stopped their cricking and the populace paused to look at the wondrous light. This capacity for appreciating the natural elements impressed me most about the Greeks. After thousands of years of civilization, then wars and occupation, the Greeks still had the ability to take life slowly and to make time for enjoying the beauty of their Homeric Land.

Those two weeks were suddenly gone. It was time to return to the forbidding grey skies of England, but as we packed our bags, I dreamed of returning to Greece, not just for holidays, but to live. I had found a spirit and a magic in the land of the Gods which had reached out to my soul.

On the plane I told Richard about my dream.
"Lizzie, why must you have a dream?"
"Because, I'm not sure what reality will bring us - that's why."

CHAPTER TWO

DISCOVERY

The impetus to change the course of my life finally came about as a result of the weather. It was the middle of May and I was sitting in my comfortable but shabby living room chair in my crumbling Victorian semi, watching the rain lashing down on the windows; I hadn't seen blue sky for months, my plan to walk on Wimbledon Common with a friend had once again been abandoned because of the diabolical English weather. The central heating was consuming thousands of units, condensation had caused severe peeling of the inner paintwork, the rising damp was climbing to unprecedented heights and I was cold and depressed. Richard had died of cancer nine years after our visit to Greece and I had missed him and grieved, but I had not forgotten my time there with him, nor my dream.

Why was I, a single (yet again), middle-aged woman, with no young children to tie me down, still living in this intemperate climate? Why was I clinging on to my stressful job as a social worker in a Conservative Borough where the financial cutbacks made the work impossible? I could no longer use my children as an excuse for staying in England. My oldest daughter Fiona, was now twenty-nine and had been in a steady relationship with her solicitous boy friend for several years now. Alison, a Graecophile of twenty-seven, was living for most of the year in Greece and had a job and a Greek boy friend. Simon was now eighteen, independent and due to start University. I could now "let go" of them and I must. I jumped up from my chair, grabbed the Yellow Pages

House in rain

and rang all the estate agents who specialised in Greece (there were very few of them then), and I asked them to send me details of houses in Greece. I did not specify a price because I hadn't got any money anyway. I had continued to visit Greece for my holidays, each time I chose a different area and islands because I could not believe that this small mountainous and ancient country could continue to surprise me with its contrasts. Each island was completely individual. The azure sky, the warm blue sea, the infinite light, the people with their humour, casualness and non-materialistic approach to life, they had got it right. This was where I would find peace of mind.

I knew the areas to avoid now. Corfu was one of them. Martina and I had spent a holiday there eight years before, staying in the beautiful bay of Paleokastritsa, which had been ruined by package tours and discos blaring every night. Paros, Tinos and Santorini were now overrun with back packers, who after an evening of drinking *ouzo*, fell asleep in their droves along the main street, a battlefield of prostrate bodies. I had also learnt that one could be stranded for weeks on the Aegean Islands because of the storms which brought ferries and internal flights to a standstill. What if I had to go to hospital or return if my children were ill? The Peloponnese was becoming overrun with British ex-pats; Germans were buying up whole villages in the Mani; The North West area was saturated with volatile Italians who dumped their detritus from their high powered sleek motor launches, leaving the sea awash with Coke cans and plastic bags. Yes, I wanted an island, but one near the mainland.

In June a list of properties arrived in the post. I searched through the house section, most of them were "Traditional

Greek Farmhouses needing some attention", which meant that there was no water or electricity, just a shell and no roof... but of course "with great potential". Then I noticed they had sent me, by mistake, their Business Section. The sales blurb read "YACHT CLUB ON SMALL GREEK ISLAND AVAILABLE". Idyllic setting, well established business. Consists of House and Taverna, fifty metres from the sea. The island of Trizonia is reached by *caique* (water taxi) from the mainland. There are no cars on the island." The price was affordable, if I could sell my house. "This sounds interesting", I thought, "I´m already on the fringe of the sailing fraternity." Apart from my part-time social work job, I was also involved with a hopelessly unsuccessful yacht swap and charter scheme. My partner, Arthur, owned a yacht which was at present based in Yugoslavia for which we employed a skipper, Jim by name; my daughter Alison was already working in a taverna in Paros and was disenchanted with the island. If it all fitted into place we could have a paying concern and a house on an island in Greece.

I phoned the agent for more explicit details which he sent first-class post. There were two photos, one of customers sitting on a balcony of the taverna/yacht club, with a spectacular view in the background of sea and mountains: the other was a picture of the village, with shuttered whitewashed houses fronting the water´s edge. The house apparently comprised of two bedrooms, a fully equipped kitchen and taverna, plus sailing dinghies, windsurfers and nearly an acre of land. Excited and tremulous I phoned Arthur to discuss my idea. Arthur is an incorrigible entrepreneur, he trained initially as an engineer, but his real love was sailing and we had started our business together as a side line, but also to enable him to be involved with yachts. He is an impetuous character and was affected by my excitement and we agreed to meet to talk things over. We did so and it did not take long for him to become enthusiastic about the idea of running a yacht club. Arthur had only been to Greece once before on a short holiday and had brought the boat over from England, through the canals to France, Italy and now it was in Dubrovnik but the charter side did not have many more bookings this year. We decided to visit Trizonia Island in late August.

Arrangements had to be made for Jim to bring the yacht "Arion Bleu" to Greece and meet Arthur and me there. I rang Alison in Greece and told her of my find and asked her if she would like to come with me. She was enthusiastic and happy to take a week off from work with Demitri, her current boy friend, and to look at my possible new business and house. However, neither Ali nor Demitri had heard of Trizonia, they couldn't find it on any of the maps of Greece. I explained that it was only three miles long and two miles wide. I arranged to meet them on a specific day at the port where Jim would, hopefully, be waiting with the yacht.

I began to doubt the existence of the island if even a Greek had never heard of it, so rang the agent, who rang the present owner who was now in England. He sent us directions how to get to Trizonia. So it did exist! This is an adventure my friend Martina would enjoy, I decided after looking at the complicated instructions. I phoned Martina and asked her if she had time to come to Greece in August?
"You know me mate", she said, "I'll finish this job and then nothing will stop me joining you, I can't wait."
So I booked our plane tickets to Athens and bought a Greek Dictionary and phrase books to improve the smattering of the

language I already knew which was limited to words like "F. Harry Stowe" which means "Thank you" and other phrases such as "No I am not interested" which I could use when accosted by hot blooded Greeks or enterprising sales people and gypsies selling plastic chairs. I revised "I am lost" as I was sure these words would be needed. I eventually found a large scale map of the relevant area which showed Trizonia as a dot in the sea.

I also collected as much information as I could from the present owners of the taverna. This included details of how to find the key to the house and explicit instructions to feed their cat (if it was still alive), which they had been forced to leave behind because of our quarantine regulations. At the end of August I locked the peeling front door of my Wimbledon semi to embark on a holiday which was to change my entire life.

Martina, Arthur and I arrived in Athens in September at four a.m. It was still dark when we landed. We could have been anywhere, but once the Boeing 737 doors opened, the heady smell of resin and the warm balmy night air hit us then it was unmistakably Greece.

We walked across the tarmac with other passengers into the almost deserted airport buildings.

"I´ll find a trolley", ever-active Arthur said. He wandered off, to return in five minutes without one. "There aren't any", he said.

"Well, other people have got them", Martina pointed out, "Where did they get them?"

I told them not to worry, I´d find one. I was, by now, aware of the idiosyncrasies of Greek airports - I went to a metal frame, with rubber flaps hanging down, where trolleys were sometimes to be found. I ducked underneath and walked outside to the cab rank, where a stack of trolleys stood on the street. I pushed the empty trolley back through the metal barrier under the flaps and into the luggage hall. No one stopped me. The customs check was on my left - but anyone could have walked through this way without difficulties. If I had been a drug trafficker I would have had no problems.

In fact the customs men barely glanced at us, it seemed it was too early in the morning. They were all bleary-eyed and longing for their habitual coffees.
"So how do we get to the bus station at this time?" Martina asked, "are there taxis around at this ungodly hour?"
By now it was about five a.m. and the first bus to the port opposite Trizonia, we had been informed left at six-fifteen a.m.
"Leave it to me", Arthur said marching across the road with our trolley full of baggage. He went up to the first taxi which was parked in a line of yellow cabs.
"Per favore, dove stazione?"
Arthur had done business in Italy and was very proud of the few words he had learnt - but he was in Greece! The swarthy bearded Greek driver eyed him up and down.
"Do you speak English mite?" he asked.
"Oh yes, right. We want to go to Kiffisou Bus Station - per favore", Arthur replied.
The driver got out of the taxi to open the boot for our bags - but the next minute the car started to roll on its own down the incline. People started shouting and just before the car was about to hit an unsuspecting priest, the driver launched himself into the driver's seat and hauled up the hand brake. Nervously, we all got into the back.
There is a saying "Most Greeks are the kindest and the most

hospitable people in the world. The rest have gone to Athens to be taxi drivers!"

Having had experience of their wily ways, I checked that he had a meter, that it worked and that he set it at the correct rate (dependent on the time of day). However, this taxi driver was honest and very voluble. He told us he had lived in Australia for seven years, running a shop, but he missed Greece so much he had to return and was now content driving in the most polluted city in Europe! The word for this love of Greece is "*Romiosini*". Time and time again I encountered Greeks who had travelled miles from their homeland to find jobs and a new way of life, but had finally returned as nothing compared to their Greece. I was beginning to agree with them.

The sun was rising, colouring the sky with vivid orange. We passed the Parthenon outlined against the sky. Athenians were starting to go to work, drawing down the canvas awnings on their shops to protect their goods from the ball of fire which would beat down all day. The smell of coffee and *souvlaki* turning on charcoal spits wafted up from every street corner. This was why they returned and why I had come back again and again. Perhaps to settle here too?

At the busy bus station we paid the taxi driver and with a "*kalo taxithi*" (Good journey) he drove off. We eventually found the ticket office, where a sleepy looking Greek man, with a coffee in his left hand and a ballpoint pen in the other painstakingly wrote out our tickets.

"Hang on", Martina said, "aren´t the seats numbered on Greek buses? We want to sit in the front. I can't sit in the back. I´ll be sick."

So she tried to ask the ticket man for front seats - he didn´t understand. Martina got out her pencil and sketchpad and

Greek bus

proceeded to draw a bus with three people in the front.

Arthur cryptically commented: "She could have just written down the numbers."

The ticket man looked at the drawing then laboriously tore up our tickets and wrote out three new ones marked four, five and six. The queue grew behind us as he motioned to Martina to draw a picture of him. She had to oblige with a very quick sketch. No one seemed to mind, in fact, they gathered round to watch and give their opinions as to whether it was a good likeness or not.

We put our luggage under the side of the bus, having asked at least six people if it stopped at our port, and clambered aboard. Slowly the bus filled up with people carrying plastic bags and parcels of various shapes and sizes. They plonked themselves down in any seat. Then someone would come along who was particular as to where they sat and produce their numbered ticket. There would be shouting and gesticulating until the illegal occupant vacated that seat.

Ten minutes before the bus was due to leave, an old man appeared. He stood by the driver´s seat facing the busload of people. He then raised his right arm which had been severed below the elbow, and proceeded to point at the stump with his left hand, all the time chanting in Greek. He then produced a greasy cap and held it out. All the passengers started fumbling for coins and put them in the cap as he passed down the aisle. We followed their example, terrified that if we didn´t, we would be cursed or have an accident and lose our right arms on the journey.

The driver climbed into his cab and immediately turned on the radio. He then adjusted his mirrors, checked his good luck charms, a picture of the Virgin Mary, a huge rosary and cross and a pin-up of Marilyn Monroe. As he started off, nearly everyone on the bus crossed themselves. I was, by now, in a terrible state of nervous tension. Should I cross myself too, to ensure a safe journey? No, I was a fatalist. I gritted my teeth as the bus swung out of the bus station, *Bouzouki* music blaring, narrowly missing a scooter on which was seated a man, woman and two children. Buses always left on time in Greece I learned. This always amazed me in a nation of people who never paid any heed to time, who would arrive an hour late for a rendezvous, or sometimes even the next day.

I was reminded of a bus journey I made when returning from a two week holiday in the Peloponnese. I had to make a three hour journey to Athens and had left myself an hour to spare at the airport before the plane left for England. The night prior to catching the bus, I had gone out with friends for a meal which went on late into the night and then on to *Bouzouki*. I caught the bus, nursing a ghastly hangover. I slept for two hours lolling against the upright Greek lady next to me, until the bus stopped at the Corinth Canal. Everyone got out for coffee and *souvlaki*. I made straight for the loo, swilled down two Disprin, sat with my head in my hands waiting for them to take effect, then wandered out to get back on the bus. It had gone!

"Shit!" I yelled, shaking my fist at the empty parking bay.

No one had come to find me, the lady I was sitting next to must have known I wasn't on the bus. I had left my hand baggage on the seat and all my luggage was aboard. As I was standing forlorn and by now crying, a young, handsome Greek man come up and enquired if he could help. I told him my sad story, that I had to catch an aeroplane in two hours time, that the bloody bus had all my luggage and tickets on it.

"*Oxi provlima*" (no problem), he said, "I will take you."

Relieved and delighted at my luck, I accepted his offer. I knew that in Greece I need have no fear of hitch-hiking, as it was standard practice for Greeks to thumb a lift. There were so many routes without buses and car owners were in the minority. What luck, I thought as I followed him to his car. I´ll arrive in comfort and in plenty of time to pick up my luggage at the bus station.

"Here we are. In you get." He pointed up to a huge double container petrol lorry! BP printed on both tanks. I reluctantly climbed into the cab next to him and we were off. He drove the lorry like a racing driver, overtaking everything in sight, careering round the bends, laughing maniacally as he did so. He smoked all the way, flicking his ash out of the window which took it backward to the Highly Inflammable load we were carrying.

"My plane doesn't leave until 2:30 p.m.", I yelled, as I held onto the handle of the door with one hand and the front of the cab with the other to prevent myself going through the windscreen.

"*Den biraisi* (it doesn't matter). We will catch the bus."

He overtook my bus, waving both hands and shouting across me "*Malaka*" (wanker) at the unsuspecting bus driver.

We careered on down the National Highway until we spotted a police car at the road junction. He came to a screeching halt. I thought the containers would surely come crashing through the cab. I was by now feeling sick. "The Wages of Fear" was tame compared to this experience.

Sir Galahad climbed down from his cab and strode over to the police. There was a conversation between them, a lot of pointing towards me and the road. They all lit up cigarettes. Then to my amazement the police proceeded to set up a block and signs in the inner lane of the road and put on their flashing lights. After two minutes or so, the wayward bus came into sight and the police stepped into the road and flagged it down. There was more pointing at me and raising of arms and shouting. Then the policeman came to the cab and with the help of the lorry driver, lifted me down.

"*Efharisto poli*" (thank you very much), I managed to gasp out of dry lips as they virtually carried me over to the bus.

"*Tipota*" (it's nothing), they said as they pushed me up the bus steps.

The bus driver seemed to think it was "nothing" too. He barely glanced my way. I stumbled to my seat. There was my overnight bag but not the upright Greek lady. Where was she? Perhaps she had left the bus at Corinth and I had maligned her. After that experience, at any coffee stop whilst travelling on a Greek bus, I have never let the driver out of my sight!

Now this bus, carrying Martina, Arthur and me was passing over the steeply cut sides of the Corinth Canal. The sea was on our right and mountains on the left, the sun was shining and I was warm for the first time in months. We stopped for our coffee in Corinth - Martina´s eyes never left the driver.

"Oh God no, now he thinks you´re interested in him", I said. For the rest of the journey he kept looking back over his shoulder smiling at Martina whilst driving at breakneck speed. The journey took several hours past olive groves, hills covered in tall cypresses - so typical of Greece, interspersed with glimpses of the bright blue sea. We passed little newly-built concrete villas all, it seemed, unfinished, waiting for a second storey, with iron rods sticking up from each flat roof. I´ve since learned that this is to avoid paying housing tax, so no new villa in Greece is ever finished.

We had arranged to meet Alison and Demitri at the port where Jim and the two girls who had helped him crew from Yugoslavia would be waiting with "Arion Bleu".

It was midday when the bus dropped us off at the port. We

staggered down to the harbour with our bags, stiff from the long journey. Before we reached the jetty we could see the tall mast of "Arion Bleu" in between the *caiques*.

There they all were. I had never met Jim before, nor the girls. Jim, lean and tanned, had a calm competent manner and was quietly forceful. Sharon and Lou, both now living in Australia were open and talkative, all of them were around thirty. Alison looked well and bronzed and Demitri was as charming as ever.

We exchanged news about our various journeys, then cast off the lines to sail for Trizonia. Alison and I sat on deck and talked all the way, happy to see each other again after so many months. The journey from the mainland, with a slight following wind, took about one and a half hours. We sighted a sheer red cliff first, then a series of green mounds rising from the sea. We hauled down the sails and switched the engine on, drew nearer until we could clearly see the first peninsula of land, which was the village of Trizonia Island.

I stood in the bows, taking in every changing aspect as the boat slowly rounded the island towards the harbour. I tried not to get too excited. There must be a snag - it looked too good to be true so far. We passed a small islet on the left and through an opening of roughly one hundred feet, with a lighthouse on the right, we found ourselves in the most perfect natural harbour I have ever seen. The land rose steeply from a little shingle beach and about fifty metres up stood the house "The Yacht Club". It was the only house there. Most of the house was obscured by almond and olive trees. But it existed!

We moored below it in crystal clear water. Martina, Lou and Sharon immediately jumped into the sea, scattering the fish round the boat.

"Come on, there will be time for that later. Let's go and get

the keys and have a look round", I cried, impatient as ever.
We left the three girls in the water and went to the village
with the dinghy, crossing the bay to the near shore. The village
consisted of a few whitewashed houses, a square with a
monument to the Greek people lost in the last war, a fir tree
in the centre of the square, three tavernas and one mini market,
its entrance shaded by a massive mulberry tree. The second
bay faced the northern mainland, which was only five minutes
away by *caique* or water taxi. Small blue and white fishing
boats were moored here, and slapped about on the water's
edge. It was idyllic. There was a large church built in the
fifties on the far peninsula, which dominated the village, and
a few children played in the sea below it.

We had been told to collect the key to the house from Xristos,
the owner of the mini market and taverna. There were about
a dozen elderly Greek men sitting around the tables under
the shade of the mulberry tree. They acknowledged us and
greeted us with "*Yeia Sou*", and I asked where Xristos could
be found. The old men waved their arms indicating inside.

Entering the taverna, which consisted of a few tables and
chairs, a bar, fridge freezer and another bar with a counter
full of sweets, crisps, cigarettes and airmail letters all muddled
up together, I saw a short, middle-aged man preparing coffee
on a small gas burner. I established this was Xristos, and
introduced myself, in my halting Greek. He motioned with
his hand for us to sit down and gave us coffee. It was thick,
strong and very sweet.
He then went to fetch the key, and came back saying (I think)...
that he had been feeding the cat, but hadn't seen it for days
now. I was really surprised that a Greek man would have
bothered to give it food, when I knew that most cats here are

First sighting of Trizonia

wild and scrounge from tables in the tavernas. They´re
certainly not kept as pets. With a promise to bring the key
back when we left, we got back into the dinghy and rowed
for the shore below the house. Sharon, Lou and Martina were
having aperitifs on board "Arion Bleu" and joined us.

We climbed out onto a boulder adjacent to a metal jetty,
which had been denuded of the planks long ago, and walked
up a dirt track road, which was only wide enough to take a
tractor. The surface was red and the soil of claylike
consistency. We reached some steps on our left, hewn into
the rock. There was a dilapidated sign lying on the bushes
which read "Yacht Club. Dinner from 7:00 p.m.". We climbed
the steps which zig-zagged and rose steeply through an
overgrown garden of grasses, thyme, sage, rosemary, cactii
and numerous trees. Arthur, having had to sit down several
times on the way, joined us later.

Suddenly there it was! A kind of wooden cabin with a balcony
of about thirty foot which fronted it.
From the balcony we all stood and gazed at the view. It was
unbelievable. In the distance were the mountains of the
mainland which fell steeply into the sea, their outlines forming
wonderfully erotic silhouettes. We could see the entire sweep
of the bay directly below us with the village to the left and
beyond, the short stretch of water linking Trizonia to the
mainland. We saw water taxis crossing in the middle.
"Oh, Mum, it´s beautiful!" Alison was the first to break the
silence.
Everyone agreed, but what about the house. The door to the
dining room was stiff, but with a bit of effort it opened and
we entered the dark musty room.
It was like the "Marie Celeste", the tables were made out of

old sewing machine bases, and chairs were set out along the room. There were yacht club flags hanging from the rafters on the ceiling. A bar at the far end still had empty bottles on the shelves, and empty glasses on the counter. There were spiders webs everywhere and an air of abandonment. The kitchen off the dining room still had crockery in the sink, the living room had a few tatty cushions thrown onto the floor, a wood burning stove, and a low ceiling with beautiful wooden rafters extending the length of it. Wooden stairs went up from this room to two tiny bedrooms with sloping roofs, in between them was a bathroom with a hip sized bath. The evidence of mouse droppings showed us that no one had been here for some time.

During our combined tour of the "Marie Celeste" I noted between the exclamations of "oohs!" and "ahs!" everyone had made some comment which intimated to me that they felt they wanted to rescue this deserted log cabin.
"We could paint over those terrible murals."
"All it needs is a new door."
"If we close this area in..."
"If we take down some of those flags it won´t be so dark."

The practical ones amongst us, Arthur and Jim, inspected the electrical and water systems. There was no mains electricity, and the generator which had powered them both was unworkable. There was a hose pipe which came up from the tanks below to the lower level of the house, the end was in a bowl, and water trickled from it. So we could get some water! There must be a pump. There were three gas rings and a gas bottle which had some gas in it, and a greasy cooker. We also found hurricane, oil lamps and candles.
We congregated on the balcony. I knew immediately that I

could live here. Everyone else loved it too, except for Demitri who, being Greek and knowledgeable about running a business in Greece, realised that the island and the yacht club were too much off the tourist track to ever make any money.

We all felt that we belonged here. The sense of discovery and the excitement which this engendered made us forget the awesome practical problems that would have to be faced if we ever ran our taverna.

Then the cat arrived. Miaowing in a hoarse, persistent way. It was thin and mangy, black, with a white front and long whiskers, and obviously knew its way around. It didn't rub itself against our legs like most cats, but just stomped around, miaowing and glaring at us. There were several empty tins of cat food strewn around the garden, though it clearly needed a good meal now, but we had nothing.

Martina rushed off to the yacht and brought back all we had, milk and salami. She poured the milk into a bowl and we crowded around to see if the cat would devour the milk. It sniffed the milk, then disdainfully marched off to the bowl of water at the end of the hose pipe and lapped from there.

"Bloody thing", Mart said. "I nearly killed myself in this heat going to get that."

Jim cut up the salami and put it down for the cat. Again, it poked its nose into the bowl then moved away, eyeing us angrily.

"Perhaps it only eats kebabs", I said.

"That's it, that's what we can call it", Alison said, "Kebab." At that, it ran to Alison and a loud, coarse purring replaced the miaowing. We learned later from the previous owners that Kebab was, in fact, the cat's name!

The thought of food made us realise how hungry we were too, so we decided to go down to the village to eat, and to buy some cat food, which presumably Kebab did eat.

This time we walked to the village, turning left along the red dirt track road with the sea on our right. The land on the left was steep but covered in green bushes, and there were plots of olive trees interspersed with almonds. No houses on this road, only a wooden shack which housed some chickens, for some curious reason there was a washing line nearby, on which hung an old pair of men´s trousers, and a plastic doll, minus several limbs. Perhaps it was the Greek´s answer to a scarecrow, but I saw no vegetables growing.

On the right we also passed a shrine. These are usually put up in Greece beside a road when someone had an accident. But as there were no cars on the island, why was it there? I learned later, after extracting truth from myth, which is characteristic of the Greeks, that a woman had fallen from an olive tree whilst collecting the crop, and never recovered, subsequently dying. The myth I prefer to believe is that she fell off her donkey whilst returning from grape picking being a little intoxicated.

On reaching the village, we made our way to the furthest taverna, because it had wooden tables and chairs and was nearest to the water's edge; it was sheltered from the sun by a large canopy. After half an hour of waiting at the table, (we were so busy discussing the house possibilities, and in a euphoric state, that the lack of attention passed unnoticed), a grey-haired middle-aged man called Spiros wandered over to ask us what we wanted. He didn't have a menu, so Demitri asked him what he had.

"Come and look," he said.

We all trooped into the kitchen at the back, where a tiny lady with a scarf on her head, stirred a few large cooking pots. There was a selection of fish, octopus, sardines, some Greek salad, potatoes done in the oven, large butter beans in tomato sauce - no menus here. We ordered our food and a kilo of the local *Retsina* wine, which was brought to us in a jug. In Greece you order even liquid by the kilo. The table was laid by a very elderly stooped man, with piercing eyes. He did everything in slow motion, first the plastic tablecloth was put on and secured by elastic around the table, then the wine was brought out, then a little later, the glasses. We started on the wine, toasting in the Greek way with clinking of glasses and "*Yeia mas*", celebrating our fortuitous find, when suddenly I noticed our waiter Spiros climbing into his *caique*, and setting off for the mainland.

Where could he be going, and why? It was obvious that our food was going to take a long time, so Demitri went into the taverna and ordered another kilo and mezzes, the little bits of food the Greeks always have when drinking. Babba Yannis (there is always one so named in any village), who was the father of Spiros, plodded out with the mezzes, olives, cheese and bits of squid on a dish.

To Demitri he said, "there is no bread, Spiros has gone to get it!"

Half an hour, and another kilo of wine later, Spiros was to be sighted returning to the island, laden with a basket of bread! So this was the pace of life on the island for the future. I loved it.

Over a very late lunch we had discussed how we all felt. We agreed that this place was special and decided we would make an offer. Demitri could not deter us.

We bought food at the mini market and strolled back to the dinghy. The sun was going down by now, behind the house, and bathing the mountains opposite in a glorious pinky mauve. Alison, Demitri, Jim and Arthur decided to take another look at the house and to feed Kebab, so Martina, Sharon, Lou and I said we would prepare some food on the boat for later on. We had a rubber dinghy and a fibreglass one so could leave one behind for the others to make their way later. It was by

Babba Yannis

now getting dark, the dinghies were moored alongside the boulder and metal jetty. Sharon got into the dinghy first, to hold it steady. Martina, maybe because she is diminutive and drink goes to her head quicker than anyone else I know, was very drunk after the strong local *Retsina* and whilst attempting to get into the dinghy missed her footing and was left hanging onto the two metal railings, by her feet and hands, with her bottom in the sea! Lou promptly rushed to her aid and jumped into the rubber dinghy but misjudged it and landed up fully clothed in the water. After much pulling and pushing and manoeuvring, they managed to get Martina into the dinghy, in a crumpled heap. There was so much relief at achieving this feat they forgot me, still on the rock, and started to leave. "Hey, you lot," I shouted. "What about me, do you think I´m a bloody mermaid!"

Giggling helplessly they came back for me.

Reaching "Arion Bleu" we tied up to it, and tried to get on board. This is not easy even when sober. You have to climb up some slippery chrome tube steps which are attached to the stern and are at a height of about two feet from the water line. "Let Mart go first", I cautioned, "so we can watch her."

She gingerly grabbed the sides of the steps and clambered uncertainly to the top step. This is where you have to change the position of your arms to grab the firm metal rail... at this point she let go completely and fell backwards into the dinghy! Luckily for Martina, Sharon who was directly below, broke her fall! The dinghy was tipping in a perilous way and I had visions of ending up in the water too. However, Lou managed to clamber out and with much shoving and hauling we got Martina back in the boat. Bedraggled but happy we went below to change. Martina, however, now naked had enjoyed her dip in the warm water and, weaving towards the steps of the hatch, threatened to go for a swim. We had to hold her down to prevent this suicide mission!

That night, in the comfort of the cabin, over a dinner of spaghetti, we all agreed that this island was a magical place. Time had stood still here. There was peace, wonderful beaches, unknown to tourists, clear sea, no cars and fumes, it was near enough to one part of the mainland to reach the nearest town sixteen kilometres away, for shopping. The bay was ideal for mooring the yacht, which could be kept here for chartering or for shopping, or enjoyment, and it was not too far from Athens to deter friends from coming for holidays. I had talked to Demitri who said the business could be built up, but he didn't want to work here. Alison did. To her it was a challenge and so different from the hurly burly of Paros. She needed a change, maybe from Demitri too.

Jim had looked at the visitors books and seen that many sailors and yachts he knew had visited the taverna in the past. So Trizonia was known to yachtsmen. He felt right about staying here and working on the house in the winter, as so much needed doing.

Arthur was over the moon as the whole place suited his ideas of running a charter scheme.

Martina said she would come back again and again to draw and bring her family for holidays.

Over all this chatter from everyone, I imagined myself sitting on the balcony each evening watching the sun going down and I knew that this was the place I was meant to live. I would never be alone with my friends and family feeling so good about the little island.

I had discovered a dot on the map which was sheer heaven, in the sun, by the sea, in my beloved Greece. Yes! I would do it. I would buy it, and change my life. How I would manage to buy it was another question.

Nafpaktos harbour

CHAPTER 3

DECISIONS

Next day we decided that Jim, Arthur, Alison, Martina and I would sail to the nearest port, Lepanto and make a phone call to England with our offer. If that was accepted we would have to visit the Public Notary to collect the necessary documents for the house to take them back to England and the final transaction could be carried out at the Greek Embassy in London.

Arthur and I discussed the price we should offer; because there was so much work to be done on the house before it was habitable we would not offer the asking price of fifty-eight thousand Pounds as we had no way of knowing if the generator or equipment worked until the owner came to Greece and gave us permission to test it. The contents were included in the price, but apart from the tables and chairs, crockery and cutlery everything was in appalling condition.

We sailed through the narrow opening between the strong stone walls which was the entrance to Lepanto. A bronze statue stood on the battlements with the inscription "Freedom" carved on the base. It was at this historic port that the Greeks had defeated the Turks in a famous sea battle. The remains of a castle stood on a hill behind the town and on the harbour wall and in the town streets, fresh spring water flowed into the fonts in a constant supply, which was vital for a town in Greece, and no doubt one of the reasons why the town was established here so many centuries ago. Arthur and I went to the nearest telephone which was in a kiosk or "*Periptero*", just beside the harbour, but on the busy road we could hardly hear our agent because of the hooting of cars and scooters. He said he would contact the owner and tell him of our offer and we arranged to ring him in two hours. We found a hotel nearby where we could telephone from behind sound proof doors, then wandered around the town trying to keep our minds off what the answer might be to our offer. Then we sat at a cafe beside the water sipping coffees and glancing at our watches. At the appointed hour we rushed to the hotel and telephoned our agent again.

"He has accepted your offer!"

"Wonderful", Ali standing beside me was whispering "What, what's he saying?"

"But it is dependent on your completing as quickly as possible, within six weeks."

"But we can't finalise until he comes out to show us if the generator and cold room and fridges are working. If they don't work then we will reduce the price to take that into account, will you tell the owner that please?"

"Of course, I'll ring back if you've got a number." We gave it to him and rang off.

"Yes, he's accepted - it's ours." By now Martina and Jim had joined us in the small hotel lobby and we were jumping up and down and hugging each other, with the mystified proprietor grinning at our un-English behaviour.

"Hold on, how are you going to pay for it?" practical Mart asked.

"Don't worry we'll find a way, get a loan from the bank, we can pay it back later out of the takings when the business gets going", pragmatic and reckless Arthur answered.

"Until my house is sold", I said, my head was spinning and I felt as though there were a thousand butterflies whirring around in my stomach.

I snatched up the phone when it rang to hear my agent say:

"Right Mrs. Parker, he agrees to your terms, and you name the price you think fair for the equipment then make the offer less that sum, then he will come out to the island when he can. You know the procedure now? Collect all the relevant documents pertaining to the house, photocopy them, then bring the originals back to England when you return. Good Luck."

"It's ours! We've done it, we've bought a house in Greece!"

"Congratulations."

We went back to the boat to celebrate with a bottle of *ouzo* and sat in the cockpit to discuss our immediate plans.

The rest of the week was hectic for me. Demitri and I went to see the Public Notary in a village fifteen minutes away along the coast. Without Demitri's help I could not have communicated with this surly, unhelpful man. He represented bureaucracy of the worst kind, only to be found in Greece. His office was packed with box files, shelf upon shelf, he did everything at a snail's pace; first he couldn't find the file, then when he did, we still had to go to the county town to have them stamped, paying for the dozens of stamps each time.

"We are the King of Stamps in Greece", stated the harassed official as he banged down the rubber marker for the fiftieth time. Armed with photocopies and stamped documents we sped back on Demitri's moped to the Notary before he closed for his siesta.

On the road back we narrowly missed crashing into a priest who, dressed in his black robes and stove pipe hat, sporting sun glasses and smoking a cigarette, seemed to have lost control of his vehicle. A moped converted into a one seater cab, with a small truck attached to the back. He had a goat tethered in the truck which had become unleashed and was dangling perilously from the rear. Demitri stopped to help

Priest on scooter

the Pappas re-tie the terrified goat and hobble its legs. The Priest thanked us, then asked Demitri for a cigarette and clambered back on his Emmett contraption. Clouds of exhaust obscured this vision as he drove erratically along the white line in the centre of the main road. I assume that because of his high religious standing he thought he would be safe from any other traffic, God would take care of him!

Finally we had all the documents and the tax dues written on a separate sheet, the Notary did not smile once and even Demitri who was used to officials declared him "The most unhelpful man I have ever met."

Demitri and Alison had to return to Paros as the season had not finished.

"I wish you luck, Lizzie", Demitri said, "I appreciate the beauty of this island, but I think you will have a struggle to make it a success, every time you need any provisions you will have to leave Trizonia, drive twenty minutes away to shop, then back again, then get from the boat to the Taverna. I have a delivery to the door and that's hard work. Alison has done a lot to make my bar more popular and although I love her, and will miss her, I know she is your family and she can and should help you."

I kissed him on both cheeks and thanked him, promising to see him next year. He pulled his crash helmet on over his curly black long hair, tears were in his eyes, I loved him for his ability to show his emotions, it was such a contrast to the English men I had known with their stiff upper lip. You knew how Greek men felt.

"Mum, I'm so happy about the house, I'll see you in England, there is so much to think about and arrange." Ali clambered on the back of the moped clutching Demitri around the waist. "Write to me."

"I will. Bye darling. Thanks for coming over."

"Could I have missed looking at our possible future? Lizzie it´s our destiny."

There were only two days left before we had to return to England. Arthur and Jim sat on "Arion Bleu" discussing the winter and plans for improving and expanding the Taverna, Lou and Sharon decided to stay for a month to help Jim with the house before returning to Australia. Martina and I explored the island, we walked along every well-trodden track, through the vineyards where the locals were gathering the grapes and laboriously filling the punnets and placing them on the donkey´s back. Then emptying the grapes into the grape press in the village.

The whole day was taken up with this work, then we watched a boy of about fifteen, who was from the village opposite, tread the grapes. A simple square brick-built container was covered with a wire frame, he ran a marathon on the top, wasps buzzing around him, until the juice filtered through an opening at the base into plastic containers. These would then be poured into barrels and stored in the owner´s house until Easter which was traditionally the time to drink the new wine. We found wild thyme growing everywhere, sage and garlic. We discovered the original water supply, a well which now contained brackish water and from which sprouted a fig tree, the luscious fruit were dropping everywhere and we sucked them as we walked along. There were no sounds except the occasional shirring of the swifts´ wings as they were startled from the scrub by our footsteps. We could lie on the beach or in the sea and hear the throbbing of a boat´s engine when it was still five miles away, so peaceful was the environment.

One day Martina was stung by a wasp or hornet on the leg. The area swelled enormously, then spread up her leg, leaving her with a red, inflamed elephantine foot which made it difficult to walk. She hobbled to the village in the evening where we sat at Spiros waiting for the others to join us for a farewell dinner. As Martina limped into the Taverna, Golfo, Spiros mother, noticed her leg. Mart did an impression of a wasp (or an aeroplane) and Golfo tutted and went into the kitchen, she returned with a very large, sharp knife, she motioned to Martina to sit in a chair then advanced upon her...

"Oh God, Liz help, I think she´s going to cut my leg off, what she doing? Stop her!", but Golfo turned the knife handle towards Martina´s leg and made the mark of the cross on the swollen area.

"Now it will be alright", she said, "thanks be to God."

"Well if it heals you ought to go and light a candle in the church."

"Listen mate, I´ll light thirty candles and offer up my children if this pain subsides."

Within half an hour the pain had stopped. With Golfo as the local witch doctor there would be no need for a "Flying Doctor" here. The nearest Health Centre we had discovered was a good twenty miles away by car or ambulance and having seen the decrepit jalopy and driver collecting an elderly inhabitant, who was tied to a make shift stretcher, hauled onto the water taxi and perilously ferried across to the mainland, I would rather put my faith in God.

Too soon came the day of our departure. Lou, Sharon, Jim, Martina, Arthur and I sailed out of the bay with backward glances at "my house" nestled into the hillside.

"We´re not abandoning you again, far from it, you will be restored to a habitable happy home by caring people, because I will never find such a setting again", I told the "Marie Celeste" as the yacht´s wake narrowed until the house was no longer visible.

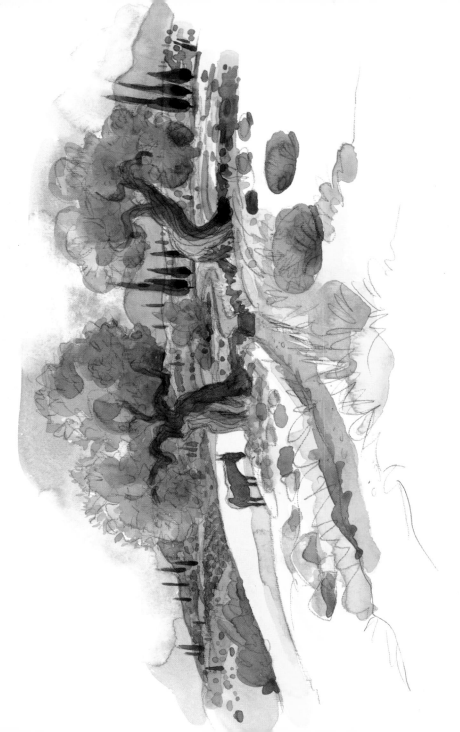

Path to the beach

The crossing to the other side of the Gulf of Korinth was smooth and a shoal of dolphins followed us for fifteen minutes, gambling and diving under the prow of the boat, so close that we could see their smiling snouts. The Greeks believe that dolphins bring luck and I felt their appearance on our last day was an omen confirming the correctness of my decision.

After our "Good-byes" to Jim and the girls, with promises to keep in touch and last minute instructions about feeding Kebab, we climbed onto the bus for the journey back to Athens. Arthur still wore his glasses tied up with string to prevent them from falling overboard, and his trousers had a hugh burn hole caused by a misadventure with a blow torch, he had two days stubble of beard. My hair was thick with salt because I had been unable to wash it owing to the shortage of water in the house and on the boat; Martina´s clothes showed white salt stains because of her frequent tumblings into the sea, but we were brown and felt healthy.

I gazed out of the bus window at the clearly defined mountain ranges sweeping down to the sea, until the bus turned right and approached the industrial area on the outskirts of Athens. In the short space of two weeks I had seen and bought a house in a country where I didn´t even speak the language, embarked on a business venture which I had no idea how to run, and committed myself to spending money I did not have to buy and repair it but, as we climbed the steps to the plane waiting on the tarmac and I turned to look at Athens in the hazy distance, I knew there was no other place I wanted to be.

I could not wait to see Simon and tell him of my find, he was enthralled with the pictures and the whole idea, he did not object to my leaving England eventually, and Greece was only three-and-a-half hours away by plane and his holidays could be spent with me whenever he chose. Because his father had left him a large sum of money, which was at present tied up in trust, I asked him if he would lend me the money to buy the house until mine was sold. He generously agreed and after negotiating with the trustees, I was guaranteed the money, with no interest! No need to go to the bank for a loan except for money to build the house extension and improvements. The dolphins had brought me luck.

I also enrolled for Greek lessons at night school, my teacher was a slight but forceful Greek woman, Lilika, who had lived for 15 years in England. She was the best teacher I had ever had, her lessons were always fun and she managed to gauge exactly what level each member of the class had reached, and question them accordingly. I would play my Greek tape in the car as I made my Social Work visits, "*Eimai, eisai, einai...*" and would frequently greet my clients with "*Yeia sou*".

Lilika came with me to the Greek Embassy in Holland Park in November when I signed the Greek document of sale for the house in Trizonia, and handed over the cheque. Everything was written in Greek, although my Greek/English speaking lawyer promised me a translation later, I hadn't a clue what I was signing, but Lilika assured me it was in order. The past owners of the Taverna grabbed the cheque and raced off to the bank with my lawyer and house agent following behind to ensure they got their percentage. I did wonder at the time why they were in such a hurry, but I had ensured that the full price had not been paid until they went out to Trizonia to prove to Jim that the generator and fridges worked. Clutching sheathes of paper Lilika and I made for the nearest pub and ordered warming brandies to combat the cold. We sat beside the mock log fire and Lilika raised her glass to wish me luck. "Liz, I think you are mad to live in Greece, I left because I had to when the Colonels were in power, but I would never return to my country forever. Why can you not settle in England where the people are less volatile and calmer?"

"I don´t know you that well Lilika, so perhaps I can answer your question by telling you about my past, then you will understand why I have to fulfill my dream and move to Greece."

"OK Liz, but lets have another brandy before you start!" Clutching two large brandies, Lilika sat down and stared at me with her dark, sympathetic eyes.

"Tell me, don´t be afraid."

"Well, alright, here goes!"

...As you know, I was born in India, that in itself is not remarkable, but what is remarkable is that I survived my childhood at all! At the age of ten months a deadly snake dropped into my playpen and as I crawled towards this new toy, I was snatched to safety from the reptile by my loving Ayah. My mother, at the time, was drinking gin and tonics at the Bridge Club. Then when I was two years old I contracted dysentery and became a puny skeleton, hovering between life and death. With the onset of World War Two I was dispatched to England with my sister to a private Boarding School, narrowly missing death, again, when the boat carrying us to the "sceptred isle" was attacked by German destroyers. All this happened before I was five. I´m sure the fact that I survived these traumatic events contributed to my becoming a "Survivor" in later life.

In retrospect, I cannot recall a time, during my formative years, when I fel t really safe, because my father then ran a tea plantation in Assam, he had to return to India, and my mother, it seemed, had no choice but to be with her husband rather than with her children. Anyway it was not considered fitting then to educate British children in India, also my mother was incapable of looking after us as she could not cook or clean, having been used to servants for many years, to carry out these menial tasks. So she went back to the demanding life of the Bridge Club and colonial life; I suspect quite relieved not to have the responsibility of an accident prone daughter. "Wednesday's Child is full of woe", she would quote at me. Thus re-enforcing my fears about what else the future might bring.

During the war years I lived a fairly idyllic existence. Our school was evacuated to Cornwall and there, apart from the occasional mine blowing up and few shipwrecks, I was unaware of the horrors of war. Hitler was just a silly man with a funny moustache.

I ran wild on the beaches, exploring cliffs and caves and learnt to swim early because I was thrown into the cold Atlantic sea from the harbour wall by an older evacuee, who disliked me intensely. My survival instinct worked again as I thrashed through the waves to the safety of the shore. Since that day I have always respected the sea and I have had a love affair with it. I love its changing hues, its power, its unpredictability; when swimming I feel an almost sensuous pleasure in its embrace.

When I was sad or lonely I would go to the sea and talk to it, and from its vast depths would come a soothing response. It became my friend and replacement parent. Despite its mercurial temperament I felt safe for the first time in my life. I knew the sea could not go away.

To overcome my unbearable shyness and feelings of insecurity and abandonment I took up acting at school. I became adept at being a different person, on and off stage. No one would have guessed meeting this amusing, confident, unruly, popular teenager, that my new persona hid a frightened child.

When my parents returned from India I was fifteen. I remember vividly the anticipation at seeing them again. My sister and I ran to meet them, for some reason the rendezvous was in the road near our school. These two small figures appeared in the distance - my mother and father! We ran to them - my sister being older and a faster runner anyway, reached them first - but somehow I managed to get caught up in a pile of blackberry thorns lying beside the hedge, I became entangled and dragged them behind me as I ran to their welcoming embrace, which I had been dreaming about for ten years.

"Whoops, here comes Wednesday's Child", were the first words I heard my mother speaking. No warm hug, no loving words, just an embarrassed greeting as I was disentangled from the blackberries which had torn my best shantung dress. But because they were back it made it easier for me to concentrate on my future, which I had decided was to be an actress. Neither of my parents showed any inclination to dissuade me from this career, although the song "Life upon the wicked stage ain't ever what a girl supposes", was common knowledge to them and most other middle class parents at that time.

I had blossomed from the puny mousy child they had last seen, into an attractive, dark haired, green-eyed adolescent. The rigours of playing tennis and lacrosse and enforced gym lessons every day had guaranteed to give me a good figure, though much to my chagrin, I had small boobs, I was not in the Marilyn Monroe, Jane Russell league, but everything was in proportion. My mother and father gave me endless hours of encouragement helping me with my auditions to drama school, not I think through feelings of guilt about having left me in my formative years, but possibly, because if I got into drama school I would have to live in London. (We were now living in Bournemouth, still by my friend the sea), and if I left home my mother would not have to cook for me. She still had not acquired that art, my father and I existed on a diet of baked beans and tomato soup. If she did produce fresh fruit or vegetables, they were always washed assiduously in permanganate of potash, as a preventative in case we should get dysentery or cholera in the borough of Hampshire. She missed India. My darling, sweet little Mama!

Years later whilst doing a psychodrama, it became clear to me for the first time, during the re-enactment, that I had preconceived ideas of what all mothers should be like, and mine did not fit into the mould. Once I realised she was a person and an individual and never could have been an "Earth Mother", all the anger, hurt and resentment I had been bottling up for years left me, it was too late then to say "I love you for you anyway", because she was dead.

I managed to get into the Royal Academy of Dramatic Art, not that my acting ability was outstanding, but because then in the 1950's, RADA was more like a finishing school. I don't believe more than five female students from my class got an acting job after leaving; the male students at that time, however, were outstanding. Timothy West and James Villiers were in my Ballet class, Jimmy for some reason always came in his slippers, Albert Finney and Peter O'Toole were my drinking partners, (Merrydown Cider only then), at the actor's pub, the Salisbury in St. Martins Lane.

Also whilst I was at RADA, I met and fell in love with an actor who had a promising future, but my parents were not impressed, in fact my mother burst into tears when told of our engagement. In this instance her instincts turned out to be correct, but we married anyway, in a church in Hampstead, with the bridegroom and four ushers all dressed in kilts (my husband being of Scottish extraction) and the tallest and most

54

handsome of the ushers was Sean Connery, then virtually unknown. Apart from being devastatingly good-looking, he was one of the kindest men I have ever met. Unfortunately I do not have a photograph of this star studded cast without the word PROOF stamped all over it, as we could not afford to have our wedding photos printed.

After a tempestuous few years of marriage I gave up my acting career to have two children. I was determined that I would never leave them to a nanny. They became the centre of my life. Of course my actor husband, who had by then become successful, needed my attention too, but I was fixated on becoming the ideal mum to my beautiful daughters, and slowly he and I drifted apart. He had made films in Hollywood and was frequently away on location, but because of our daughters I could not always join him and did not want to subject them to the dangers or discomforts of life in the desert and jungle. However, when he was in England I was included in the company of mega stars. Robert Mitchum remains my favourite individual, unconventional to an extreme. The first time I met him with my husband at his Dorchester suite, he opened the door dressed only in a tie! With great difficulty I kept my eyes on his decadent face. Robert Shaw, Richard Harris, Richard Burton, James Stewart and many other famous and infamous actors were frequent visitors to our rented flat in Kilburn. But despite, (or because of) this glamorous lifestyle, after the proverbial seven years of marriage we drifted apart and the marriage ended in a bitter divorce.

At twenty-eight I was alone with two children of three-and-a-half and one-and-a-half. Luckily my survival instinct was still with me. I was fortunate in having a house to live in, but realised I needed to work, not for the money only, but in order to find an interest outside the home which would prevent me from dwelling on the bitterness I felt about being abandoned again and having to give up my acting career.

I answered an advertisement in "The Evening Standard", a marriage bureau was seeking... "A sympathetic, older woman as an interviewer". What an opportunity! If I got the job, my immediate and desperate thought was, that I would find another husband. I got the job, but not a second husband (not straight away). There was a great shortage of eligible men at that time and I was forced to match six foot amazonian women with five foot jockeys, but I loved the work and the people who employed me.

The majority of the women I interviewed were sad and lonely and, as many were single parents, naturally I felt a sympathy for them. It was because of my contact with so many women in the same situation as myself, that I began to develop a social conscience. In the theatre I had led a vapid existence in a world of fantasy with no thought for social conditions, politics or real poverty, but because of the personal situation I found myself in, having to bring up two small daughters alone, coping with their demands, their illnesses whilst working, trying to give them love and security, I became increasingly aware of the disadvantages single women experience. I was also very angry at having to renege on my intention to bring them up myself, but had been forced to employ a mother´s help although I only worked part-time - I determined to rectify the plight of one parent families - but not yet.

I had been living alone for seven years, this doesn´t mean I was celibate, far from it, but none of the men I had met possessed the qualities I sought. Then I met him. It was through the marriage bureau, which had been computerised, and I was helping at the launching of the first "Get Together

Party". No need now for the "matching up" in date form, instead all clients were flung together in a bar in Central London, warm sweet wine and canapes were handed round by the staff. Everyone wore a label stating their name, making introductions less formal.

This novel idea did not take into account the myopic hopefuls, who came without their glasses, in order to appear as attractive as possible, (contact lenses were not then generally affordable). They would peer too closely at the man's jacket and then mistakenly say "hello there Tim" for "Jim", or "Len" for "Ben", or "Victor" instead of "Hector".

Luckily I was not short sighted so when I noticed a tall, blue eyed good looking man staring at me over the heads of a gaggle of women, I smiled back.

My employers were not very happy that I disappeared with the only really eligible man on their books. They were hoping to use him as bait for the next advertisement, but they came to our wedding a year later. I was five months pregnant at the time, but to make amends for stealing their number one prize, I let them print a wedding photo (from the shoulders up) in their advertising literature, captioned... "You too can find happiness forever through the Cupid Computer Marriage Bureau".

It didn't turn out like that for me, not the "Forever".

The happiness came at the birth of a cherished son after a difficult Caesarian section, and the security provided by a then, loving husband. Also a significant episode at that time was my first visit to Greece on my second honeymoon. I tried not to compare it to the first honeymoon when I had spent one night in a seedy hotel in Croydon. The moment I arrived in Lesvos, or Mytillini, as it is commonly known, I felt that I had been to Greece before, the sense of déjà-vu was so strong.

I did not believe in past lives, I just knew I belonged.

The warmth caressed me, the air enlivened me, the vivid light, which I have never seen in any other country enchanted me and I was back to my beloved sea, and this time a warm one where I could float for hours with my enceinte stomach protruding above the surface, wallowing in the divine heat of the sun.

I had visited France, Spain and Italy occasionally on brief holidays with the children and enjoyed the different cultures, but I had never experienced this sense of belonging elsewhere, this contentment. Nor had I before been able to communicate with a race of people whose language I knew not a word, at such a basic level. I wanted to stay forever, to steep myself in the atmosphere, I realised then that I had never really adjusted to life in London. I made a vow that I would return to this country, but it would be five hard, harrowing and traumatic years before I saw Hellas again.

With a husband at home to share the responsibilities of the children, I decided to pursue my interest in social problems and completed a diploma in sociology at night school and then found part-time work with a welfare organisation specialising in one parent families. The appalling living conditions of some of these courageous young women in areas such as Brixton and Balham meant that I buried myself in other people´s problems, rather than looking at my own. Mine were immense.

My second husband had developed cancer of the bladder. After a year of being treated with conventional medicine and surgery he decided to turn to alternative help with the rigid Gerson Therapy. This entails preparing fresh organic vegetable and fruit juices in a special grinder, every four hours. I stayed at home to help him with the diet, but even after six months it did not cure the cancer, his mental attitude at the time could have obviated his recovery, and the cancer spread to his lungs. I was with him when he died. I shall never forget the horror of his death. He was a skeletal figure, dosed with morphine, his chest rattled so loudly that you could hear it in the next room. I lay down on the bed beside him to try to sleep - suddenly there was silence and I knew he was dead. I had never witnessed death before and I was in total shock.

My son was away on a school holiday at the time, when he returned he asked "Where is Daddy?"

I gently told him. His huge brown eyes stared at me unbelievingly, then his thin nine-year-old body started to shake. I took him in my arms and into bed and he sobbed all night, until finally exhausted he fell asleep.

After nine years I was alone again. I was training to become a qualified social worker which meant that I had to analyse myself before I could think of helping others in a professional manner. I recognised that the events in my past, the losses, abandonment, the fear of rejection, the inability to express my innermost feelings, the bottling up of resentment, all these factors had created an anger within me which I had dwelt on throughout my forty-five years of life. I attended psychodrama sessions fortnightly, alongside my other work, to enable me to find an answer to my questions but by then it was too late, the unexpressed anger had created cancer in me. I had cancer of the cervix, which spread to the uterus and then after a hysterectomy the biopsy showed that there were still cancerous cells in my body. I attended the Marsden Hospital in the Fulham Road, there I spent nineteen hours in a closed ward, legs in the air with a radioactive isotope up my fanny. I don't know what else to call it because there wasn't much else left.

Alone and very afraid I found myself believing the common credence that I was paying the price for my promiscuous past by having this inhuman phallus inside me, I never wanted to open my legs again. But the treatment worked. I attended the Marsden regularly for check ups, then after a year when the euphemistic "down below" was clear, they discovered I had breast cancer.

I now believe that this final discovery was the one which made me change my way of life. Only when you are faced with the possibility of death do you realise with clarity the false premise on which you have based your values.

Fate brought me in touch with a woman who had also had breast cancer and been told she had two months to live. Two years after she was able to give me the telephone number of a miraculous doctor in Harley Street, who was also a believer in homeopathy and alternative medicine. I made an appointment and was shown into a room which resembled a greenhouse rather than a surgery. A tall straight backed man with the bluest, most piercing eyes, took my hand and sat me down. I told him my history, medical and personal.

"My dear lady", he said, "no wonder you are unwell, but you can get better."

He put me on a strict vegetarian diet, I had weekly injections of the healing substance which is found in mistletoe, I wasn´t to drink or smoke and ordered to rest for two hours every day, without a book, my mind completely still. I followed his diet, I didn´t find that difficult, giving up smoking and drinking was. I was given time off work and had an operation on my breast to remove the malignant cells. I have nothing but praise for the staff at the Marsden, they knew I was on a diet and encouraged anyone who was following alternative medicine together with conventional surgery, which was for me actually necessary.

Throughout this bleak time I found that the love and encouragement of my friends and family was the force that carried me through. My children nursed me, respected my new life style and were patient and strong. And my friends (a lot of them there were, I realised), showed me compassion and love. It was their outspoken expression of love for me that convinced me I "was" a lovable person. If they all loved me so much why could I not love myself?

I had time to relax and I read avidly, particularly books on self-healing, The Simonstown Method on Positive Visualisation, the Louise Hay book of affirmations and I practised their pioneering techniques. I read and re-read Shirley MacLaine's books, and discovered the New Age concept. I discussed crystals, energy and meditation with many friends who were also seeking the true essence of life. My intuition told me that the only way to find a way to heal myself in total was to search for my inner self, to discover the truth of my reality. Shirley MacLaine had done it by going to the remote region of Bhutan in the Himalayas. I knew I wasn't able to find that sort of peace while I was living in London, but I could not afford to leave work.

"But now I know I have to take a chance. Lilika, I have not yet had the opportunity to find the "wild side" of my nature, you have had your time in Greece, I believe that only by living there I will get in touch with my real self, that intuitive, creative part which seems to have disappeared since I have lived here."

Lilika took my hand, "Now I understand you Liz, *"Sto Kalo"*, (go to the good), and I will come and visit you when I have my holidays. Shall we go?"

As I struggled through the crowded bar filled with suited city gents relaxing after a day's work and heard the familiar

English tones, "What'll it be old chap?", "A pint of Guinness thanks", I wondered how much I would miss the English genre and habits. The blast of cold air and flurry of snow which enveloped us as we opened the door into the street dispelled my sentimental thoughts.

If I had not been fortified by the several brandies, which by now were coursing through my veins and creating an effective central heating system, I could have turned into a snowman. It could never be this cold in Greece.

"Lilika you're the mad one", I said as we braced ourselves to reach the protection of the warm Underground.

CHAPTER 4

IS IT WORKING?

We had set an opening date for the taverna on the fourteenth of April, and we had to have our holiday brochures, (which had been effortlessly and artistically designed by Martina) printed in England with the accompanying leaflet, setting out the dates available for the rooms as we needed to distribute these to prospective clients. The house only had two bedrooms but we planned another two below on the first balcony. This meant a concentrated working party and pro-fessional building expertise.

Jim agreed to do the building work over the winter until the charter season started in April and he enlisted the help of a friend, Nick from England, to assist with the heavy construction work.

Alison found a girl friend Mickey who was also a graphic artist, but out of a job and disenchanted with her life in Lon-don, to help her. Mickey was dark, pert and very pretty, they were a complete contrast. They left on the "Magic Bus" for Greece in February, this arduous journey took three days, I saw them off at Euston in the freezing cold, two beautiful twenty-five year olds, one dark, the other fair, who were excitedly chattering about their plans for the taverna and the journey ahead.

They clambered aboard a super Pullman coach and I waved a gloved hand at them until they disappeared from sight, shouting "Good Luck Darlings".

And did they need it! On arrival in France after crossing the Channel they were allotted another coach, not a Pullman but a clapped out coach with one driver who looked as though he was about to fall asleep at the wheel and beside him lay a bottle of brandy which he swilled down at very regular intervals.

The journey through Yugoslavia (which was then open to outsiders) became a hazardous nightmare with snow and ice covering the mountainous roads. After three days and nights they arrived shattered and dirty in civilized Athens.

"Oh, Mickey, thank God!" Ali breathed. "At last I can go to a decent, proper loo, that porta-cabin bucket on the bus put me off, I haven´t had a shit for three days!"

She sped to the lavatory at the bus terminal whilst Mickey collapsed on to a bench surrounded by their rucksacks and graphic materials. An hour passed, but no sign of Ali.

"She can´t be needing any more time to relieve herself", Mickey thought. "What is she doing?"

Mickey asked an old lady in black, who was also surrounded with parcels, to look after their luggage and went into the loo. She heard Alison shouting from the last cubicle.

"Help, someone help!"

From under the door ran a torrent of water and Mickey saw Ali´s feet under the gap.

"Ali, what´s up?"

"Mickey! Come in, the door´s open but I can´t move."

Paddling through the water Mickey pushed open the door to find Ali sitting on the lavatory seat, leaning forward with the metal cistern draped across her shoulders.

"Shit, darling, what did you do?" Mickey queried.

"All I did was pull the chain and the whole bloody lot came off the wall. Greek plumbing is the pits! Can you get the cistern off me please."

Struggling and heaving Mickey managed to release Alison

from her cumbersome load and they waded out of the loo, soaking wet and slightly hysterical about their anomalous introduction to Greece.

On arriving in Trizonia they were greeted by Jim and Nick and also an Australian couple Darren and Helen, both were in their early twenties and were on their way around the world. They had met Jim in Patras and it turned out that Darren was a professional carpenter, which was just what we needed to make the doors, window frames and beds. They were delighted to find work and the money to subsidise their European travels. Jim and Nick had already built the balcony below and roughly constructed the rooms. The house became like a beehive, buzzing with activity. The outside was painted white, and the shutters dark green, the asbestos roof was coloured the same rust red as the slates on all the other houses in the village; inside, the walls were whitewashed, the floors and woodwork varnished, curtains were hung, signs were made. One huge one running the length of the roof so that yachts people could see "LIZZIES YACHT CLUB" as they sailed into the bay. Other signs at the bottom of the steps and the jetty read "TAVERNA NOW OPEN". Above the door of the taverna "LIZZIE S YACHT CLUB" informed clients that they had found us at last. The graphic artists were determined that these eye catching signs would attract customers in the coming season.

The end of March arrived and instead of the "Marie Celeste" a clean, gleaming little house and taverna stood smiling at the first signs of spring. The "workers" were joined by a girl-friend of mine, Jenni, who had just had a hysterectomy and needed a rest. However, because she is a very competent and practical person, also kind, she joined forces and framed mirrors, painted doors and collected pebbles every time she walked to the beach, only white flat ones, to put on the many steps leading up to the taverna. Ostensibly this was to enable customers to see their way up or down at night, as there were no lights on the path then.

The evenings were spent huddled round the small wood fire in the back room as it was still cold in the mornings and evenings. They would roast jacket potatoes, drink *ouzo* and discuss the work programme for the next day. Ali would make her customary list - a habit which she and all my children have inherited from me. It became a source of amusement and everyone would crowd round to see what tasks had been allotted to them before they fell into bed. Darren, Helen and Jim were still sleeping on the boat, because although the beds had been made we still had not bought the mattresses. Darren, like many Australians, liked his drink, and after two *ouzo*s too many one night, while trying to negotiate the first bend of the steps on his way to the boat, fell into a large cactus. He was pulled from the offending Triffid, cursing and swearing and Helen spent the next few hours pulling thorns from out of his nether regions. He was off work for two days.

Everyone was enthralled with the island. The spring flowers, harebells, poppies, and crocuses were blooming, the almond trees were a mass of pink blossom, the wild asparagus sprouting. There were trips to be made on "Arion Bleu" to buy stones and cement for the foundations and garden and there were many trips to the beaches where they collected driftwood for the fire and more flat stones.
There are three beaches on Trizonia which are accessible on foot, and a map was drawn, by Jim, of the island and pinned onto the notice board so that guests would know where to go. Red Beach on the far west side of the island was so named,

Wood burning stove

because all the stones were red due to the rock formation which was of quartz and gave the area a reddish sheen, and I always felt a spiritual energy when resting on the glittering shingle.

On the south east was a beautiful cove sheltered from all but the south wind, by two rocky promontories. Unfortunately, after the winter storms it was covered with jetsam and plastic bottles galore - it had to be called Bottle Beach.

Then further round to the south was a beach and several small coves where capers grew and it was from here we had sighted dolphins in September, gambolling and diving. So Dolphin Beach this became, not original, but it meant something to us and when the summer came, we would leave notes "Gone to such and such beach", this was essential information in view of the unexpected winds which blow up out of the blue on this stretch of the Mediterranean, particularly if we had gone by boat.

The main problem in running the taverna was to produce enough power for lights, fridges and for pumping up the water. There was a diesel generator at the back of the house which was hopelessly temperamental. It had to be run twice a day to provide enough power for our needs. When running, it made a loud coughing sound which reverberated round the otherwise silent bay and it was virtually impossible to sleep when it was operating.

Water to the island came from a mountain spring on the mainland, via a pipe laid along the sea bed, then it was stored in a well above the village. Our water pipe was fed from this and it came through a metal pipe along the road and entered three base tanks at the bottom of the garden. From these it had to be pumped up every day through a plastic hose into two top tanks; there was a constant need to check the level to see they were not overflowing. This antiquated system was unreliable and time consuming.

So Ali applied for electricity, which had only been brought to Trizonia ten years before. She made many visits to the nearest, equivalent Electricity Board, which eventually resulted in an official and his minion appearing at the house to discover what we needed. They established that we would need ten wooden columns from the last house in the village to carry the wire to the taverna. No, they didn´t know how long it would be before we had any lights, but wanted a large deposit, the equivalent in drachmas, of one thousand Pounds, this was to be deposited with the bank before anything was started.

Ali phoned me anxiously.

"Mum have you got the money? We must have electricity, it´s impossible to run an efficient business without!"

This was in February. We raised the overdraft and sent a Bankers Draft for thousand Pounds to the National Bank of Greece, confident that some action would be taken. It was not.

So poor Ali struggled on planning menus, discovering the cheapest and best places to buy provisions and, of course, drinks. The logistics of getting anything to the island, then up to the taverna proved to be arduous and impractical. Everything had to be brought to the mainland opposite by taxi or lorry (if the yacht was not available), then by water taxi round to our jetty below, unloaded and dragged up a sheer set of steps, then put on to a cart, designed by Darren and inappropriately nick-named "The Rocket". It consisted of a wooden cart on two bicycle wheels, with one metal handle at the front end and two metal handles attached to the rear. The Rocket was then fastened at the front to Alison´s even ricketier old Moped and with someone pushing behind the load would be taken thirty metres up the steep dirt track road to the bottom of the steps leading up to the taverna. The provisions then had to be physically carried up the thirty five steps into the shade of the first level terrace. It took all day to carry up the crates. We were lucky in still having the yacht available and Ali, Jim and the others sailed off to the nearest port to stock up with crates of drinks before "Arion Bleu" was booked for a charter. The deck was covered in Coke bottles, Sprites, orangeade, soda, tonics, beers and crates of wine all strapped down to prevent them sliding into the sea which was still very rough in March. This beautiful yacht became a cargo boat but undertook her new role with style and patience.

The beginning of April came too quickly, last minute purchases were made of mattresses, pillows, crockery, saucepans and Ali stocked up on food, herbs, spices, napkins and loo paper from a supermarket in Athens in preparation for the first customers.

The kitchen was equipped with a three ring gas burner, a very old gas stove, (bottled gas) which had no oven regulator, a microwave which we had smuggled in from England, as such items were prohibitively expensive then in Greece. There was a very old chest freezer, which made sick gurgling noises, when it was run, the mornings and evenings only, otherwise it produced huge glacial formations preventing us closing the lid. There was also a second hand fridge freezer. None of these could be run all day for fear of the generator over taxing itself.

But Ali and Mickey got used to all these idiosyncrasies and they were very organised despite the lack of efficient equipment. They had decided to provide international cuisine,

70

"Arion Bleu" crates aboard

apart from the usual Greek starters, because the main complaint from everyone who had visited Greece, was the lack of choice of food in the tavernas. "Chili con carne", "Liver and Bacon" and "Thai Chicken Salad" were to become the house specialities, and baked potatoes, as opposed to chips with everything. There was always a dish for vegetarians and cheesecake or fruit and yoghurt for puddings.

We would be catering mainly for customers off the yachts as there was no lighting on the rough road to the taverna and Greeks are loathe to walk anywhere, but we hoped we would also attract local people even if only for drinks and mezzes. Greek people are usually very suspicious of any "foreign food" and generally ask for their traditional fare. If they are adventurous enough to taste a different dish, they will smother it with salt and lemon, thus eradicating any "haute cuisine" effects.

Arthur had contacted a large English company specialising in flotilla holidays in Greece; they were based on the Ionian Sea and would be sailing past Trizonia at the end of April. About forty yachts in all and he informed the manager that the Yacht Club would be open to all their customers. They would definitely stop at the island, particularly if we had liver and bacon! So we knew we had at least seventy customers at the beginning of the season and Ali wrote "FLOTILLAS ARRIVE" on the relevant date of her calendar, and secretly hoped they would not be the only ones.

Later Arthur informed her that he had ten bookings for holidays in the house which meant there would be revenue from those customers, with breakfasts and lunches served until two p.m. Of course the guests could eat wherever they wanted, but we anticipated that the walk in the dark to the village might deter them. Ali decided to open a Post Office account.

In England Arthur and I were rejoicing over the fact that we had four yacht charter customers. They were in the main, friends, and the very expensive adverts we put in the yachting magazines every month did not produce any response. Perhaps people were suspicious of this small outfit with only one yacht available, based in an area no one had ever heard of in Greece before.

We spent more on adverts than we ever received from chartering, but as we were doing everything on a tight budget we could not afford to employ the expertise of marketing companies. I composed travel instructions with Do´s and Don´ts about getting to Trizonia for those eager clients who had booked their rooms. It was a difficult place to reach if you were unfamiliar with that region, and everyone was, so I went through the journey methodically, setting out the difficulties on arrival. Taxi journey to bus station, bus journey, ferry and water taxi and final destination. This was sent to the guests after they had paid their final money. I showed the print out to Martina as she had also drawn the map on our brochure.

"God, Lizzie, you can´t give them that!" she remarked, "No one will want to go to Trizonia after reading it. It sounds a terrifying journey, and look what you´ve put about the taxi drivers, "Untrustworthy, check their meters, and call the police if trouble", that´s enough to frighten anyone off at the onset! Also, just because you had an unfortunate time on a bus, because you were hung over, it doesn't follow anyone else will be left behind."

"Look Darling, it´s printed now, and better safe than sorry", I tritely countered.

"What the hell did you ask my opinion for?" was Mart´s fair rejoinder.

However, I thought we had better have a taxi service all the way to Trizonia for those rich enough or tired enough from their plane journeys to warrant such luxury.

I contacted Ali to ask her to find a local taxi driver who would take our bookings. Ali asked in the village where she could find a taxi, there were three assigned to the local area only, but the driver with the biggest car, an old Volvo, was Yannis. She visited his house on the mainland and was told by his stout, sharp featured wife that Yannis was in the *Kafenion*. Ali trailed back to the waterside cafe and enquired which of the assembled, intent card players was Yannis the taxi driver.

"That one drinking *ouzo*", the proprietor pointed a grubby finger at a large square-faced man with black curly hair and a lined face.

"*Yeia sou* Yannis, I´m Alison from Trizonia", Ali introduced herself. He rose to his feet and beamed at her grasping her hand.

"*Yeia sou Koritsi, Wou... ou li...a. ou?*"

Ali was incredulous at the voice which answered her - it was a strange croaking sound which kept breaking off before the end of each word so you were left having to guess the actual meaning of the sentence. Despite Yannis´ impediment he was a friendly, kind and eager man, and agreed on a set price for our customers. The problem was how to book him as she could not understand him over the telephone, so had to write down the times and date of arrival and printed a card which said "LIZZIES YACHT CLUB", so Yannis could display this at the Airport. He was very proud of the sign and carried it in the boot of his car wrapped in a tablecloth. Yannis was so good natured that even when a customer rather stupidly put his cigarette butt out of the window and it blew back inside the car and set light to his hair, he just smiled benignly as the client beat him about the head to extinguish the fire, thinking, no doubt that this was some English custom.

The trouble was he spoke no English either, and because of his voice, even if the guest knew a few words of Greek, they could not communicate with him: but worse, he would breathe fumes of *ouzo* over them on meeting and this meant that they spent the whole journey frightened of his driving ability. After three and a half hours of travelling, (the last hour consisting of hair pin bends, and where at each corner they saw monuments erected to those who had died in car accidents), our customers would arrive in a state of terror and exhaustion. In England I had given in my notice and the house was still up for sale, but no definite buyers yet, so I planned to let it if I couldn't sell it and move out to Greece anyway in June and live on the rent until a deranged purchaser wanted my Wimbledon semi.

I decided to go to Greece for the Festivities at their Easter time; my son Simon and two close friends from my social work days were also coming out to be paying guests, to give us a financial start to the season and because they wanted to see my "folly" and to discover what had induced me to make this metamorphosis so late in my life. Arthur was to come by car trailing our second hand "Dell Quay Dory" boat and engine through Europe and to arrive two days after us. He also had plans to cram the car and boat full of items which would be difficult to obtain in Greece such as spares, tools, VHF´s and a few items of furniture which I could not bear to part with, such as an old apothecaries chest, which I felt would be in keeping with the style of the house and also be useful for keeping ants and mice at bay. The Royal Marsden Hospital had told me I did not need a check-up for another eight months and I was sure that my resolution to leave England and enjoy a different life style was an integral part of my recovery. Stress was a word I would forget.

Monument

CHAPTER 5

A GREEKISH EASTER

Simon and Sue, my friend from London who had previously accompanied me on my holidays to Greece, and I were met by beaming Yannis, the taxi driver at Athens Airport at five p.m. Greetings and hugs proved to me this time that he had not been at the bottle, so we settled into his old Volvo for the three and a half hour drive to the island. It was dark by the time we reached the jetty opposite to take the *caique* to the house. I was excited and bursting with anticipation as to what I would find, I had not, until then, seen any of the changes, only been informed by letter or phone.

As we rounded the peninsula in the dusk with the lighthouse flashing its helpful signal, I was overwhelmed with the enormity of the task Alison and the others had undertaken in order to make the "Marie Celeste" into a Yacht Club and a business concern, and also filled with trepidation as to whether I had even done the right thing in buying it. But the vision which confronted me dispelled my latter thoughts.

The house, which is set on the hillside facing the bay, has thirty-five steps; Alison and the others had heard the sound of the *caique's* engine and were coming down the steps with hurricane lamps and torches, zig-zagging spots of light revealed their procession down to the new rough stone jetty to greet us.

"Darlings, hello. How are you? Let me look at you."

"Simon and Sue how are you? Great to see you again."

We stumbled up the pathway with Mickey, Jenni, Jim, Helen, Darren and Alison lighting the way to the house which they had transformed in the space of two months. Arriving at the front door I gasped at the newly painted and orderly dining room, everyone was clamouring around, their faces showed that they were eagerly awaiting comments on their endeavours.

"Well Mum what do you think?"

I couldn´t say anything but slumped into a chair with tears pouring down my cheeks.

"Does it look that bad?"

"No Darlings, forgive me - I just can´t believe I am here at last - that you have created this place out of the ruin I first saw and that it will actually be my home. Thank you."

To avoid their embarrassment at my emotional display they busied about showing us the other rooms.

Simon gazed about him murmuring, "It´s great, Wow, awesome."

"Oh, Lizzie I love it, you´ve done the right thing, what a heaven!", Sue said enthusiastically.

We sat down at the long wooden table to eat. Exchanging news, listening to the problems they had encountered and discussing plans for the future.

Several *Retsinas* later I felt tired so excused myself and climbed the curving wooden staircase to my small bedroom under the slanting roof. I got into the newly made bed between the fresh sheets, there was no sound outside except for the gentle lapping of the water below. It was the first time I had slept in the house and I could hear it saying to me: "Welcome, relax, you are safe here", so relax I did into a peaceful sleep.

The next day Arthur and Nick were expected to arrive with the "Dell Quay dory". From the balcony we could see the mainland and Simon sat with the binoculars focused on the place where Arthur would launch the boat.

Whilst waiting I inspected the house, marvelling at the changes and particularly at the lower level balcony which had a new shower room and loo, where you could shower with the door open looking at the sea, trees and flowers, it had to be the most beautifully sited loo in the world.

Arthur and Nick arrived on the mainland after spending the night in the car. Arthur in his excitement to launch the boat and wanting to cut a dashing appearance with the engine racing across the bay, forgot to put the plug in the bung hole of the "dory". They started to sink fifty metres from the far shore! Luckily one of the local water taxis saw their plight and sped to Arthur's rescue. The engine of the "dory" could not be started, so Arthur made an ignominious entrance being towed behind the *caique* into the jetty below. We all helped unload the boat and the car's contents then Arthur set about mending the "dory" engine. He was always happy when tinkering with engine parts so I left him to relax in the way he enjoyed most.

By early afternoon he came wheezing up the steps, "Well, Liz I fixed it, shall we go for a spin?"

"Why not, let's go to the island opposite."

We set off in T-shirts and shorts, the twenty-five horse power engine started easily and we roared off to the beautiful island outside the bay, a distance of about one and a half kilometres. When we were approaching the shore of St. Georges Island the engine suddenly stopped. Despite Arthur's frantic efforts to start it, nothing happened, so we rowed briskly to the beach before the current took us out into the open sea. We waded to the beach, gasping with the coldness of the water which was up to our thighs, and tied the boat to some wood. Arthur had left his cigarettes in the pocket of his shorts and they had got wet when he was in the water so he put them out to dry in the sun, then proceeded to take the engine apart.

I set off to explore the island confident in Arthur's mechanical prowess. The island was very verdant, a derelict house was crumbling in a small bay and a tiny unused chapel beside it had been made into a bar by some enterprising Greek. There was a charcoal spit and signs written in cracked paint on the chapel wall "*Souvlaki*, Coca Cola, Ice Cream. Welcome to the Monastery Bar", who could have allowed this sacrilegious act in this strongly orthodox country, I mused, as I picked my way through the pine cones and cactii and back to the beach. Arthur was looking very despondent.

"What is it?"

"We´ve run out of petrol!"

"Shit, what do we do now? No one even knows we are here." Arthur blinked and reached for a sodden cigarette to light, but the lighter didn´t work! I left him rubbing two stones together in a frantic effort to light a ciggy to sustain his craving. He hadn´t thought of lighting a fire to attract attention as well.

It was getting cold and the wet T-shirt and shorts were not warm enough now in the late April afternoon, so I climbed round the bay to a rock which faced the mainland where I could see the water taxis ploughing backwards and forwards. I found a white polystyrene box and then stood on the cliff waving in the manner of the distress signal I had been taught at my short time in "Basic Sailing Theory".

After an hour my arms were numb but I saw one of the *caiques* diverting from its normal course and making for our island. I climbed back to the beach to find Arthur, still trying to light a cigarette, and told him the good news. Once again he was towed back to the house and, to his mortification, by the same *caique* which had come to rescue him earlier.

Easter in Greece supersedes any other Festival in the country, the build-up starts at Lent with Orthodox Greeks fasting and

Priest with child

not touching meat, oil or fish. The Good Friday ceremony is a moving and traditional time when the representation of Christ´s body laid on a bier is carried round the village and laid in the local church. Saturday night, prior to Easter Sunday is the culmination of the festival when everyone gathers together and crowds into the church with their unlit candles. We all walked to the church in a light drizzle before the midnight service began. It was packed with the villagers and we acquired our candles and stood at the back of the church, drawn into the atmosphere by the dramatic tones of the priest chanting the Liturgy; the ornate lights, the icons, and fascinated by the locals in their best clothes who stood or sat transfixed by the Deism.

At midnight the Priest said "Christ is risen", and the bells started to peal, everyone in the church turned to each saying "Christ is truly risen", and then we followed their example as they lit their candles, first from the Priest´s, then each other´s.

As we struggled to go out, shielding our candles from the wind and rain, fireworks exploded all around us in the paved area surrounding the church. The children shrieked with joy and lit fireworks dangerously close to us, I then understood why the word Pyromaniac comes from the Greek, because the adults then followed the children´s example. We left the bangs and whistles and unpredictable "Made in Hong Kong" pyrotechnics and made our way up to the house, as tradition demanded, with our lighted candles. A lucky year is predicted if you can get home without the candle going out. Because of the rain and wind few of us managed to accomplish this, but we relit our candles at the door and made the mark of the cross above the entrance with the snuffed out candle.

There were many invitations from the villagers to join them in the traditional Easter Day meal, so we ambled down to the village at about one p.m. The rain had stopped and in the square sat ten men all turning a makeshift spit of iron over a metal barrel sawn in half, filled with glowing wood and charcoal. On each spit was a skinned kid (Katsigaki), its head still attached, bronzing slowly over the flames.

"Mum, it´s enough to turn you into a vegetarian" said Simon, (and he did give up meat).

He had seen the tiny white kids previously on the island, gambolling and skipping beside their mothers, whose udders would be touching the ground before being milked in the evenings. I had already become a vegetarian but this was the only time I would eat meat.

The Greeks would rise early on Easter Sunday to prepare and cook the traditional meal of *Kokoretzi* (the entrails and liver of the kid), which was made into a sausage shape and also cooked on the spit. They were so insistent I ate it and could not understand my strange vegetarian ways on such an occasion, so I accepted a morsel, but they watched me till I ate it awaiting my reaction to the culinary delight, so I couldn´t even throw it away.

By the time the kid was cooked and taken off the spit with the head chopped off and left to drain in a bowl, most of the locals were too full from *Kokoretzi* to eat the animal. The meat was sliced off in great chunks, the head kept for picking at and the wine flowed until the dancing started at five o'clock. The men showed off their prowess, towel, dish cloth, kerchief, whatever article was handy they used in the traditional circular dances, then one man would take centre stage and jump and bend in a graceful flowing motion. It was difficult to accomplish sober let alone after several carafes of strong local wine. Anyone and everyone who wanted to would suddenly rise and join in. Shouts of »*Ela, Bravo, Xronia*

Polla«, were heard above piped music. Children ran around carefree and happy. Looking at them then, I realised that here was a race of people who knew how to enjoy themselves without affectation, completely spontaneous in their actions and I had perhaps chosen to be amongst them for this reason. At nine o'clock when the elders had nodded off in their chairs, the games of *Tavli* were brought out, the embers in the fires were barely glowing, so we thanked our hosts and with our torches made a disorderly procession back to the house.

"Mum, I did enjoy the day and the atmosphere and my first Greek Easter - but those poor little animals - Yuk!" Simon said blearily as he went to bed.

That day was significant in his juvenescence as it changed his way of thinking about the course that he would pursue. An experience on this remote island shaped his future too.

We were joined after Easter by my other social worker friend, Joyce and her son Paul, who were accompanied by a Greek mainland couple Maria and Vassillis, who she had met in London. Joyce is an outgoing, warm, and lively woman and her appreciation of the house and island was voiced in positive terms. She and Sue walked every day to some part of the island, with their walking boots on and sticks in their hands, they discovered tracks through the olive groves and scrub land leading to areas which I had not been. Paul and Simon lounged around as teenagers do and tried out the wind surfers and lasers, but the sea was too cold for water sports. Vassillis and Maria had never been to Trizonia before and proclaimed that the island was "totally unique", even with their knowledge of Greece.

Arthur and Jim prepared "Arion Bleu" for the charters which were booked, the first one being at the end of April, a family of four who were to sail without Jim.

Alison and Mickey concentrated on stocking up the taverna

whilst they had the use of Arthur's car and also whilst they had more people to make a human chain to bring the heavy drinks crates up the thirty-five steps.

Jenni and I gardened every day, re-planting geraniums, cutting back the long grass so that the snakes we had seen would be more discernible, hacking away at the hard stony soil with pick axes to try and create a vegetable patch where we would grow herbs and lettuce. We had smuggled in plants from England which were not easily found in Greece, such as comfrey, evening primrose, honesty and honeysuckle. We managed to terrace a small area at the side of the house, it was on a steep incline, but the only possible site. With the help of our newly made friend Ileas, from the village, we ordered ten sacks of manure to improve the soil. The goat manure, (he assured us this was the best) was brought by the shepherd, Takkis, from the village visible on the mountain mainland about six kilometres away.

This same shepherd would bring his flocks of sheep to Trizonia to graze when the grass in his region had been depleted. He would coax the sheep into Ileas' small blue *caique* at the jetty, wielding his shepherd's crook with the curved handle, and making strange whistling noises, then Takkis and about ten sheep, all jammed together and frozen with terror, would chug over to the island. They scrambled off "Baaing" with relief. He would make this trip about ten times and not once did a sheep fall into the sea.

However, I witnessed an even rarer sight when Ileas and Panayotis tried to get their donkey onto one of the water taxis. The larger *caique* was run by a good looking, usually immaculately dressed young man, Lambros, he was fastidious about his boat, always cleaning and polishing it.

This particular day he was on duty when they tried to get the donkey onto the bows of the boat. They pulled and shouted at the animal who refused to budge, the whites of its eyes showing, its hooves dug into the jetty.

Ileas and Panayotis then proceeded to tie its four legs together and with help from the other passengers, lifted the donkey bodily onto the small bow of the boat. All the other passengers had to sit inside. The sea was rough that day and the poor animal swayed perilously at the front. On reaching Trizonia, the donkey's legs were untied and as the two men jumped out on to the harbour wall to pull the donkey ashore, it excreted a pile of steaming turds on to the boat!

Whether it was fright or just out of spite for the experience to which it had been subjected, I will never know, but Lambros's face was a study - disgust, fury and disbelief. He shovelled the offending turds into the sea, (with no thought for someone like me, who could have used it for my veggie patch), got out broom and bucket and swabbed down the deck with manic fervour, until not a trace of the dropping was left. He shouted at Ileas, that he would never let his donkey on board again. I'm sure the donkey smiled as he was lead away, knowing now he would never have to undertake that journey again.

Then it was time for me to leave. Simon, Sue, Jenni, Joyce, Paul and I were returning to England via Athens, re-tracing our original journey on the bus from Lepanto, over the narrowest stretch of sea on the crowded ferry, clambering back onto the bus to drive the three hours on the southern shore, to the teeming capital and then to the International Airport. Vassillis and Maria had already left and Darren and Helen were to continue their travels in Europe. Arthur and Nick had to drive the car back to England.

We left Ali, Mickey and Jim at the village after a large and soporific lunch. They were more confident in their abilities to cook and organise the running of the Taverna and were

Donkey with twigs

waiting the arrival of the flotillas to bring in some more money. They had tested out the dishes on me and my friends and we had given honest opinions as to the quality and we Guinea Pigs were still alive. The flotillas should have impeccable service and gastronomic delights awaiting them.

More than anything I wanted to stay, to be in the sun by the sea and in the fresh air, to be part of the life here, but I had to work out my notice, say good-bye to my clients and colleagues and sell the house to raise enough money so that I could live in Greece.

If I invested the capital from the house in England there should be enough money to provide me with a basic income for my needs, which would include - food, bills and clothes - well I wouldn´t need many of those in the heat, bikini, shorts and T-shirts were the normal attire. I would also have to have enough for the up-keep of the car which I intended buying.

Alison was capable of managing the Taverna and she would use the income from the meals and drinks to pay Mickey on a commission basis, which was the usual way of paying staff. Arthur and I would take any money made from the letting of the rooms to pay bills, fuel for the generators and the boat and insurance on the house and general expenses. Jim´s salary would come from any yacht charters we could find.

But now I had to return with Simon, who was at University, to find him a base in London. All this had to be done before I could think of moving permanently. I could not make another way of life until these factors were settled. Despite my ability to do nothing for hours on end, I can only really relax when practical issues have been resolved. I had "let go" of my children, I now had to "let go" of all that had been familiar to me for the last twenty-five years.

CHAPTER 6

THE OPENING

Alison and Mickey, with Jim helping as waiter and "washer upper" were prepared for the arrival of the flotillas now expected at the end of April.

Twenty charter yachts sailed into the bay throughout the afternoon. The lead crews consisted of the skippers, the engineers and "Hosties", who would see the yachts into the harbour and ensure they anchored safely, then with our newly acquired VHF, Alison would welcome them and ask if the "Hostie" would like to know what was on the menu and perhaps give her the number of clients for dinner.

The majority of the lead crews were Australians or New Zealanders, nearly all in their twenties, bright, fit, and energetic, they bounded up the steps with no shoes on, bronzed, usually attractive and with their casual manner and enthusiasm endeared themselves to the girls straight away.

"Howdie Mate, get the stubbies out of the ice box."

Settled with cans in their hands they would have the assembled company in hysterics recounting the exploits of the inexperienced yachties or "punters", who were perhaps chartering for the first time.

Ali managed to ascertain that there were forty people coming for dinner, they would all arrive together and the skipper would "brief" them about the plans for the next day, discussing charts, hazardous rocks and weather conditions, then they would eat at the Taverna.

All the tables were joined together running the length of the room, places were set, salads prepared, *Tzatziki, Humus* ready and bread cut to be placed in baskets. The generator was running at full strength, fridges and ice box pumping, the lights would dim when all the electrical machines were working, but surely no one would mind, it would add to the romantic atmosphere. The main meal would be prepared on the gas burners and potatoes were baking slowly in the oven. With confidence, Ali, Mickey and Jim waited for the onslaught.

The "Hostie" preceded the forty hungry sailors who stood on the balcony at first admiring the view, then sat down to order drinks and await the food.

Then it happened!

The gas ran out! The spare cylinder was empty. Jim abandoned his role as waiter and kitchen hand and lugged the cylinder down the steps and into the dinghy. He whizzed over to the village to purchase a full cylinder and panting brought it into the kitchen so the main meal could be prepared.

The customers were now relaxed after a few drinks and having eaten some starters did not notice the hiatus in the service. Ali, muttering darkly sweated over the now hot burners, plopping baked potatoes, chili con carne, liver and bacon and chicken onto the plates which Mickey would whisk away. "Nothing else can go wrong; not tonight."

Indeed, apart from a minor incident when Mickey was carrying a tray of steaming chili con carnes to the tables and a small gecko dropped into a bowl from the ceiling above, (to be deftly extricated by Mickey with a fork) before serving, all went smoothly until the main course had been consumed.

The sound of laughter was predominant from the replete and slightly tipsy, satisfied customers. In the kitchen Ali and Mickey hugged each other and patted Jim on the back as he scraped the left overs into the bin.

"Well done all of us" crowed Mickey, "We've dealt with our first invasion."

Then the lights went out!

Shrieks, oohs, hysterical laughter, ghost impressions filled the Taverna. "Roger, get your hands off me", "Where´s my wife gone?", "I´ve lost my specs."

Jim resourcefully lit a couple of hurricane lamps whilst Mickey lit candles and they were placed on the tables amongst the debris of glasses and bottles.

Ali who was left in the kitchen noticed a smell of burning from outside, "Jim, help, the generator, have a look quickly!" Jim sped into the garden, torch in hand to discover the ancient generator on fire, the flames were spreading to the trees and bushes behind the house, he rushed into the Taverna, "All hands on deck."

His nautical training and common sense was, thank God, still very evident. He organised the befuddled and bemused customers into a human chain in the garden; passing buckets of water from the tanks nearby to quench the fire which was encroaching onto the house, sizzling and hissing when the water splashed over it, the burning wood gradually lost its terrifying heat and became a black trail of smoke. The fire was out, but so was the generator.

The customers, grimy from the smoke but still good humoured were offered drinks on the house and as they sat over the candlelit tables it seemed from the general conversation that tonight´s episode superseded all their previous nautical tales of mishaps.

They even promised that they would be back in October on the next delivery trip, just "In case we needed their help again!"

"How I appreciate the stoical English", Mickey said, now relaxing with a glass in her hand, as the last retreating customer swayed through the door.

"Yes, but what now? No generator, so we have no lights, no

fridge, no freezer and no more water. But you know why it caught fire? Because we got carried away with the events of the evening and we forgot the golden rule - NEVER HAVE MORE THAN ONE MACHINE PLUGGED IN AT THE SAME TIME. We had the fridge, freezer and cooker on - plus lights! Oh shit! What am I going to do with all the food in the freezer?", Ali looked desperately at Jim´ll fix it.

"Ali, let´s not think about it now, it´s late, I´m exhausted as you must be, tomorrow when you´re fresh it will seem easier."

"Yes, I suppose you´re right, anyway, look at all this money! Drachmas galore, if business goes on like this we have nothing to worry about."

Ali stashed the takings into a shoe box under her bed, they exchanged "Good nights".

"Thanks so much for your help, both of you. What a team we are, pity we have to rely on engines too."

Exhausted they all went to bed with the acrid smell of smoke wafting on the still night air.

CHAPTER 7

THE CLOSING

Over a strong coffee on the balcony next day, with the sun rise long past, Jim, Mickey and Ali discussed the best strategy to take...

"Without the generator and no power we have to close, nothing else to do."

"But all the food in the freezer will go off."

"Look Ali, cook it all today and then ask Thanassis in the village to put it in his freezer."

"Yes, brilliant idea, then it will be ready for customers when we eventually open."

"But what about getting the generator fixed, surely that´s a priority!"

"You´re right Mickey, I´ll go down to the village and find out if anyone knows a Suzuki specialist nearby."

"Someone ought to ring Mum and ask her to send a bank draft for the repair - and by the way, the first paying guests for the rooms arrive in two weeks time, we´ve got to have the generator working by then!"

Ali and Mickey cleaned up the taverna as best they could with no running water, then started to cook the mounds of meat already thawing in the useless freezer. Jim took the dinghy to the village and found Xristos sipping *ouzo* at Thanassis.

"How goes it Jim?"

Xristos had taught himself English and he liked to practice it with us - but only if it was not too early in the morning; it was past eleven o´clock and the *ouzo*s had made him approachable. Jim recounted the saga of the generator and luckily Xristos

knew of a specialist in the town Eqhion on the south side of the mainland. He obligingly loped off to telephone from the metered phone at the back of the taverna. Although there was a door to enable one to have more privacy, people rarely closed it so the whole village was aware of everyone's private lives and tribulations.

Because the majority of Greeks phone from *peripteros* (the small kiosks which sell cigarettes, sweets and newspapers), which are found on busy street corners and with a cacophony of traffic noise around them, they all shout into the phone. It doesn't matter if the phone is situated inside, the habit is ingrained. So shouting into the phone Xristos told the mechanic our problem, whilst the old men in the cafe nodded and grunted over their coffees about the news regarding *Oi Angloi*, from up the hill. We were the topic of conversation for that day.

"Jim, you can take the generator with the yacht tomorrow and he will repair it for you", Xristos said, "I'll help you dismantle it, the girls can't lift it."

"Xristos thanks so much, now I have to phone Liz."

Jim rang me and I said I would arrange a bank draft as soon as he had an estimate from the mechanic. I reminded him of the guests arriving soon and sympathised with him but agreed they would have to close. I suggested that Ali go directly to the equivalent of the Electricity Board known as the DEH, and ask them when they were going to start work on bringing our supply. We had registered last September about needing a supply and deposited one thousand Pounds as surety with the National Bank of Greece, confirming our veracity, but we had heard nothing and we weren't even getting any interest on the deposit.

"Right Liz, I'll speak to you again." Jim rang off and sped back to the house to give Ali and Mickey the news.

"Good old Xristos, what would we do without him, my Greek

isn´t good enough to deal with mechanics and such specialist talk", said Ali.

"I´m no further than *Oxi* and *Nai*, Mickey added.

Actually she even got *Oxi* wrong, saying it with a nasal twang which sounded more like Oinki, as though imitating a pig, but she said it with such charm and with an accompanying smile that everyone would crease up.

"I´m going to fetch Xristos later to help me take the generator down to the yacht."

"Jim, can you wait a little, we will be finished with the cooking soon and we can take it over and ask Thanassis to store it at the same time. I´ll ask him if I can do him a favour, like some signs as I will have time if we are closed."

Ali had been long enough in Greece to know the general maxim - "one favour deserves another".

An hour later with all the cooked food neatly parcelled in plastic bags of various sizes, they took the supplies over to the village. Mickey guarded the food for fear of the wild cats taking a leap aboard to have a feast, while Ali found Thanassis loading crates into his *caique*. He agreed that Ali could use part of his huge commercial fridge until we could get the generator mended. Hastily the precious supplies were carried into his taverna and placed to one side of the freezer. Over another coffee Ali and Mickey agreed to do a large sign over Thanassis´ door with his family name; with another sign stating "This way to the mini-market".

Thanassis was a very enterprising young Greek and the only waiter I have ever seen running to tables to serve customers. The whole family worked extremely hard and the business was open from seven a.m. until after twelve p.m.

Jim had found Xristos and they all went back to the Yacht Club to help dismantle the generator and to haul it onto the yacht for the trip across the Gulf of Korinth. The closed signs were put up, the taverna locked and Ali painted a rough sign and attached it to the bottom gate.

DUE TO UNFORESEEN CIRCUMSTANCES THE TAVERNA WILL BE CLOSED FOR TWO WEEKS - WE DO APOLOGISE.

"What a way to start the season", Ali said glumly as she and Mickey hammered the sign across the gate.

"Do you think it will be two weeks?"

"Look Mickey, I´m going to sit on the doorstep of the DEH night and day until they do something."

"Well that means I´ll have to do the signs", rejoined Mickey, "And I can´t speak Greek let alone write it!"

"Don´t worry I´ll do it in rough for you."

"Have you also thought about how I´m going to see, we will have no lights."

"Work in the daytime and we´ve got candles and lamps for the evenings for ourselves."

Alison has a stubborn streak and refuses to be beaten by most events and her time in Greece had also taught her to take all disasters in her stride. They waved to Jim and Xristos as "Arion Bleu" sailed out of the bay with its precious cargo.

The first week Jim phoned the "Specialist" Suzuki engineer every day to check on the progress of the repair. There were "difficulties" Jim was told, then there was an ominous silence. The "Specialist´s" telephone remained unanswered for three days.

"Why?", Jim enquired of Xristos.

"It´s a holiday, a Saints Day - don´t know which one."

Xristos could be very obtuse when it suited him, but we soon learnt that these Saints Days were very frequent and each village and town have their own named Saint, to try to do business on such a day was an anathema.

Time after time they wasted hours travelling to remote villages, which for some idiosyncratic reason housed the Tax Office, the Town Hall or the DEH, all in different inaccesible places - arriving to find them closed.

Alison went to the Manager of the electricity company in another remote town and pleaded and cajoled, lost her temper and then dissolved into tears. The latter must have moved the implacable bureaucrat, because he picked up his pen and said he would order the ten columns to be brought to the island... soon... no mention of electricity, but the columns were the big item and he would guarantee their delivery. Alison was to look out for them within the next month. Wearily she caught the last bus back to the mainland, but pleased to have accomplished some positive action.

Mickey completed the signs for Thanassis` taverna whilst Ali was away. She painted on to a nine foot board, the name "*TOMATO YANNIS*" as she put the brushes into the white spirit Ali came stumbling up the steps to the balcony where the completed sign was lying on the floor.

"What the fuck is that?"

"I thought I´d surprise you, is it OK?"

"Mickey NO, actually it isn´t. Oh my God!", and she collapsed, laughing hysterically, into the nearest chair.

"Well I copied what I thought you´d written, but your writing is so awful - anyway he must sell tomatoes!", Mickey sheepishly and quite immaterially countered.

"Look Mickey its "*STAMATA YANNIS*", his surname, anyway don´t worry, now it will go with all the other classical mistakes to be found all over Greece on signs and menus."

Alison and I had spent many joyous times collecting and annotating the errors in graphics all over Greece. Whenever we were given a menu (these only being available in tourist places, in small villages the local owner told you verbally what he had or asked you to step into his kitchen); we would scan with delight the listings.

The classic mistakes to be found in most tavernas were, "LIMP SHOPS" for lamb chops, "MINGE MEAT", for mince, "LOMSTER", "SHRIMS", "GREEN FIELDS", which must have meant Horta, and in Sparta I once saw "INKWELLS" for kalamari. Then there were the other classic tourist signs... "FOUL BREAKFAST", instead of "Full", and "INGLISH IS SPEAKEN ERE", "ROOMS FOR FREE", and unaccountably, a sign on the edge of a remote and stagnant lake which stated - "NO NUDDING. THIS IS CIVILIZATION". It was inconceivable anyone would want to swim there, let alone nude!

That week a forty-five foot yacht flying an Australian flag sailed into the bay. Despite the "Closed" sign a large rugged man with his equally large wife struggled up to the taverna. "Hello there, I´m John and this is Angie, we´ve come all this way to find you and now you´re closed. Any chance of a beer then?"

"Well, yes, we can give you a beer but it´s not cold."

"What sort of place is this then? Greece and no cold beers! No worries, it´s not that hot anyway. Let´s have two."

John manoeuvred his large frame onto a chair and Angie said; "Is it any trouble?"

They chatted freely about their sailing experiences and life. They had left Australia six months before having decided to let their flat in Brisbane and to sail round the world before they were too old. They were only in their forties and John was very fit. Angie had back problems and also had skin cancer, so she wore voluminous shifts to protect herself from

The Tomato Man

the sun, but she was a warm, outgoing lady who just got on with life. To earn extra money they had bought with them an old sewing machine and generator so Angie could mend sails. They were interested in the life in Trizonia and wanted to know how Alison coped with a business in such an isolated place.

"With difficulty", Ali told them, "one of the problems is the lack of electricity and our generator has broken down, that´s why we´re closed and you´ve got warm beers."

"No, I can´t believe it", John expostulated, "two English Sheilas having to do all this manual work", he was really chauvinistic, but delightful despite it.

"No we´ve got Jim to help us some of the time, when he´s not on charter and he knows a lot about mechanics."

Just then Jim appeared with a grim look on his face. Introductions were made, then Ali enquired as to the reason for his sober look.

"The generator is not ready and the bastard will not give me a date, he keeps saying something about not being able to get the parts."

"Shit, we´ve got the paying guests coming next week, what are we going to do?"

Angie who had been listening attentively turned to John "Perhaps we can help these folks Doll, we are not using our generator at the moment and we´d gladly lend it to tide them over."

"Yes, sure", John agreed. "It´s slightly under powered for your needs, but you would have light and a fridge for our beers!"

"Would you... could we borrow it?"

This generous couple took Alison under their wing. John connected the generator and the lights, though dim, worked, but more importantly the fridge and freezer worked and the water pump. John enjoyed helping and was very practical. Angie loved cooking and had many recipes which she shared with Ali. They intended coming to Trizonia for a week, but ended up staying three months!

With the reassuring sound of the burring motor behind the house, the food was repacked into the freezer, the water was now pumping into the house and the Closed sign taken down in preparation for business again and the arrival of the paying guests.

The columns had still not arrived from the DEH, but we had enough power to provide a service of sorts. Beds were made up in all the rooms, towels laid out, everything was sparklingly clean and neat.

Breakfast times were set out on the Menu... 9-12. Lunch 12-2 p.m. and then the afternoon would be free for swimming or whatever they wanted to do.

Jim was expecting his first charter clients and would be away for two weeks, so the girls prayed everything would run smoothly, at least until he returned.

CHAPTER 8

THE CUSTOMER IS ALWAYS RIGHT

Greece in May is still fresh, the grass is green and in the field opposite goats grazed amongst a sea of poppies, the sun was warming and the snow on the mountains around the island had melted, only one high peak on the mainland to the south was crowned with a white cap. The sea shimmered enticingly, but was still too cold for swimming, except for those intrepid hardy Brits who were to be our first paying guests.

"Here they are!"
Mickey peered through the binoculars from the balcony at Xristos's *caique* rounding the rocks. A couple were perched on the bow gazing up at the Yacht Club. Ali and Mickey hurried down the steps to welcome them at the jetty below; a stocky, white faced and clean shaven man in his late twenties, jumped on to the land and extended his hands to his new bride to help her off the boat. She jumped into his arms and they clung together perilously swaying on the edge of the jetty before regaining their balance.
"Hello, you must be Frank and Eunice", Ali greeted them as they reluctantly unravelled themselves from their embrace.
"Yes, how do you do, phew what a jouney, poor Eunice is shattered, aren´t you dear?"
Eunice blushed and became even pinker than her shocking pink suit, her huge blue eyes stared up at her husband and she breathlessly whispered, "Oh, but Darling it doesn´t matter, we´ve got a whole fortnight to sleep!"
Xristos handed their matching suitcases with in-built wheels

from the boat and was paid the fee for bringing them round, then Ali and Mickey led the way up the stony road. Frank struggled up with one suitcase then returned for the second. Eunice was having difficulty climbing up as she was wearing inappropriate high heeled shoes which kept buckling under her, and the wheels on the second suitcase had broken on a particularly sharp stone.

Mickey showed them to their immaculate room above the kitchen, explained where the bathroom was and warned them about putting the lavatory paper down the toilet.

"How quaint and rustic", Eunice remarked. "But we don´t mind, after all we are in another country now - when in Rome..."

I had other less charitable thoughts when I first visited an island in Greece on a package tour at the beginning of my infatuation with the Hellenes.

On the way from the airport to our apartment whilst the tour operator had us all seated on the bus, she told us the general information we should know about the area and then said, "Oh, and please make sure you do not put your toilet paper down the lavatory."

She then went on to talk about local customs.

"Well, what do you do with the lavatory paper - eat it?"

I wondered as I gazed at the other passengers who were looking equally mystified.

Frank and Eunice went to bed. They didn´t get up very often except for meals and the occasional stroll to the beach. Ali and Mickey spent a lot of time in the kitchen and could hear the squeakings and murmerings from above. Then one day the carnal sounds reached seismic proportions and at the height of cavorting and presumably a climax, there was the sound of splintering wood and a HUGE CRASH! Mickey

Xristos´ *caique*

and Ali exchanged meaningful glances to the heaven above and continued chopping vegetables. Several minutes later a bashful Frank knocked o n the door.

"Er um, excuse me, so sorry to have to tell you - but the bed has collapsed! Frightfully sorry and all that, don´t know what to say..."

"Please don´t worry, we´ll get it mended, they are not very strong anyway", said Ali tactfully, but she remembered Darren´s habitual taste for *ouzo* and wondered if he had in fact made the joints properly.

Eunice hovered in the back-ground, still as white as the day they had arrived.

"Perhaps we´d better go to the beach for the day darling", she ventured, "until the bed is mended."

"Good idea sweetheart, a change is as good as a rest."

"Not that you´ve been doing any resting", Ali remarked as they departed.

She and Mickey collected hammer and nails and did their best to repair the bed until Jim returned and before the lustful honeymooners came back from the beach.

Jim sailed back at the expected time with the repaired generator on board. John and Angie who had been waiting to take a short trip to the Ionian Islands, helped replace our mended generator and took their own back to their boat. They decided they would leave in a few days, but would return after a week as they loved Trizonia and were happy being around the Yacht Club and chatting to the other visitors at night. Then, before they left, Ali received a letter from the DEH to say ten columns for the electricity had been delivered on the mainland opposite. A council was called, John and Angie of course were included.

"Look, if we get the columns over to the island the DEH

won't have an excuse to delay putting them up and then connecting us", said Jim listening to the hiccoughing of the generator.

"Tell you what mate, we've got two yachts, lets tow them over and leave them below on the beach."

"My thoughts exactly", said Jim. "We'll need plenty of good strong rope."

The family who had just chartered "Arion Bleu" for two weeks had decided they would also like one week ashore and had booked accordingly. The Maddox Family consisted of middle aged parents - Anne and James - keen sailors, but somewhat ineffectual people, who were holidaying for the last time with their surly teenage son and daughter - Kim and Charles, who, typical of that age group, showed no interest in their surroundings and lolled around with Walkmans on their heads bemoaning the fact that there wasn't a disco for miles. They had been requested to take their clothes off the boat as they were now sleeping ashore.

Then Jim and John up-anchored and motored out of the bay to pick up the huge wooden and creosoted columns, they lashed them together then looking like some Canadian Lumberjack specialists, slowly towed them back to the shallow waters below the taverna, where they were rolled to the safety of the beach, and secured to the nearest trees. The villagers had watched this feat with enjoyment and obviously respected Jim and John's enterprising spirit. They were very aware of the long wait for electricity.

The disposal of rubbish was also a problem on the island. There was a haphazard service run by a Nico Triantafilo (Mr. Rose), black plastic bags would be left at the corner of the road to the village and Mr. Rose would stop, pile up his tractor and trundle to the rubbish dump which was half a mile away on the other side of the island. Because the taverna produced more rubbish than a single household, Ali would often attach the "Rocket" to her decrepit motor bike and then would bump off up the track, the "Rocket" piled high with plastic bags and empty bottles. This day she decided to do a rubbish run, because she was expecting not only the Maddox family, but two other clients.

"I noticed some rubbish on the beach by the jetty", Mickey told Ali. "Bloody Yachties, dumping their rubbish there, how do they expect us to dispose of it?"

"Not easily, I'm going to put a sign down there", said Ali as she set off on the bike, collecting the offending black plastic bags from beside the jetty on her way.

Several hours later Ann Maddox appeared at the kitchen door, "Mickey, we've been settling into our rooms, but we seem to have mislaid some of our clothes, or rather the children have."

"Sorry, Mrs. Maddox I don't know what you mean."

"Well the children left two bags of dirty laundry - clothes we'd used on the yacht in two black plastic bags by the jetty."

"Oh, really - well I'll talk to Ali about it and see what's happened."

Mickey already guessed, but she had to discuss the mistaken cleansing operation with Ali. She found her in the shed painting a sign in red which said "PLEASE DO NOT LEAVE YOUR RUBBISH HERE; TAKE IT TO THE VILLAGE WHERE IT WILL BE DISPOSED OF".

This was not entirely correct, because although Mr. Rose ran a service, it was erratic, so most of the villagers threw their rubbish into the sea; chicken heads, plastic bottles, iron bedsteads. old chairs, shoes, all would be tossed in, despite a sign in the village square, "HEALTH IS CLEANLINESS. KEEP OUR SEA CLEAN", it told us in Greek.

"You know what you've done Ali? You just happen to have

taken the Maddox´s clothes to the rubbish dump, those two bags by the jetty, well they were full of dirty washing and they have very few clothes left after two weeks on board."

"Oh, no! Look maybe Mr. Rose hasn´t collected them yet, I´ll go and see if they´re still there."

She sped off to the corner disposal, but, for once Mr. Rose had completed his redolent and arduous job early. Only a few cats were around picking at the left over food.

Mrs. Maddox and family were sitting on the balcony and the teenagers were looking even more surly having been told off for their silliness at leaving the bags on the beach.

Ali approached them warily, "We are so sorry but because so many people leave black plastic bags by the jetty, we assumed your clothes were rubbish, and I´m afraid they´ve now been taken to the tip."

"My best jeans", wailed Kim.

"What about my designer labelled shirt and jumper?" Charles bleated.

"Can I suggest you take a walk to the rubbish tip, it is a really beautiful part of the island, and see if you find them amongst the rubbish", Ali gave them a ravishing smile.

"Jolly good idea, we havn´t walked anywhere for weeks, come on chaps, lets get ready."

James, the father, pushed the children up the stairs. Five minutes later the family reappeared. They were in trousers, yachting boots, heavy weather oil skins and round their faces they had tied handkerchiefs over their noses and mouths.

"Perhaps you should take sticks as you might want to poke about in the refuse."

Mickey produced four sturdy bamboo poles, "Good Luck then."

"Heigh Ho, Heigh Ho, it´s off to work we go...", James chanted as he led the way on their bizarre expedition. The teenagers were not singing. Two hours later they returned with James dangling one black sock from his grimy hand. "No luck I'm afraid, the digger had been down before us and covered most of the refuse with soil - but it was an enjoyable walk."

After making the right noises Ali suggested they could claim off their insurance. They did just that on their return to England and we had a letter from them saying the insurance company had accepted their story and paid up. I suppose even an insurance company could not believe anyone would invent such a story.

John and Angie left in their steel hulled boat promising to be back in a week (in case we needed them).

"Don't worry, we've got the repaired generator", said Ali, without much confidence. All the rooms were let for a week and a couple of English ladies were expected that day.

"Have a great time, see you in a week."

The English ladies were to be met by Yannis at the airport and driven back to the mainland by 11 am. By 4 pm there was still no sign of them, so Ali phoned Yannis at the Ouzerie, shouting down the mouth piece at him when he got to the phone.

"Yannis, what's happened? Where are the ladies?"

"I go tomorrow for English ladies."

"No, Yannis it was today!"

Ali cursed herself and Yannis for not checking thoroughly, but realised she was fighting a losing battle with the *ouzo* bottle and determined to use the soberer Ileas in future.

On her way back to the "Dell Quay dory" she saw two well dressed older women pulling their suitcases behind them on trolleys, they were obviously English and very dishevelled and dusty, Ali approached them enquiring if they were Mrs. Taylor and Mrs. Fortescue...

"We were when we left England", the smaller dumpier one with rinsed blonde hair replied. "But that was so long ago I could have taken on another identity!"

They explained to Alison how they had made their way to Trizonia after Yannis had not appeared, via bus, taxi, bus, ferry and then eventually hitch hiking to the mainland jetty. These two matronly looking women had guts and stamina and were blessed with a wonderful sense of humour. Alison's apologies were brushed aside as they recalled their adventure and giggled about their introduction to their Greek holiday. For two days Dixie and Annie, (Mrs. Taylor and Mrs. Fortescue respectively) brought gaiety and hilarity to the atmosphere at the taverna. Even the Maddoxes, who would sprawl for hours on the balcony, doing nothing, were encouraged to move and the teenagers took off their Walkmans and went swimming and walking. Evenings were spent playing "Trivial Pursuits" with Dixie and Annie gulping their way through strong Martinis. They never saw the dawn breaking over the mountain; always rising late and ordering Bloody Marys with their brunch!

On the third day after their arrival Mickey was preparing breakfast when Annie put her head round the door, she had a towel draped round her neck and her hair was covered in shampoo.

"Mickey dear, there doesn't seem to be any water to rinse my hair with."

"Oh, Annie, sorry I forgot to start the generator to pump up the water this morning, won't be a minute."

Mickey climbed up the slope to start the generator, she pulled the starting cord, but nothing happened, she checked the oil and fuel and tried again. Still the engine spluttered then died. Ali came up to try, but it would not start, so they yelled over the balcony at Jim on the boat below. He rowed over then came up to tinker and fiddled about, unscrewing all the working parts thoroughly, but the 'repaired' generator would not start. James Maddox, a self confessed DIY man had a go, but there was not a spark of life.

Meanwhile Annie sat on the balcony with a large Bloody Mary whilst Dixie took photos of her friend with clotted hair. Ali, Jim and Mickey had a conference behind closed doors in the living room.

"You know what this means? No water, no loos, no fridges again", Ali started beating the cushions on her bed. "Shit, shit, shit!"

"We will have to move them out to the hotel, ring Liz and ask her if they will compensate them for the inconvenience and will Liz and Arthur pay for the remaining time in the hotel?"

"Only thing to do, but they've all had to put up with so much already. Thank God it didn't happen when the honeymooners were here! I'll go and tell them, would you ring Mum Jim, she has to say "Yes"."

The paying guests assembled outside, Dixie and Annie giggling happily and Ali offered free drinks all round and told them of the plan.

"We are so sorry, but we know you will like the hotel, its very modern, they have electricity and running water, we of course have to check there are rooms, but it's not usually full at this time of the year."

"I don't think I want to leave", said Dixie, "I feel really at home here. We can all fetch sea water up for the loos and swim and wash in the sea. We can eat in the village or you can cook by candlelight."

"But Dixie you won't have any ice for your Martinis", ventured Mickey.

"Well then I'll have *ouzo* instead."

"Here, here", said Annie. "But could I go to the hotel just to rinse my hair?" They refused to budge.

The Maddoxes however, (and particularly Kim who washed her hair every day) decided to move.

"And be sure not to leave any dirty washing in black plastic bags", Annie ordered as they went upstairs to pack their few clothes, yet again.

When Jim rang me and gave me the cost of the rooms at the hotel which he had ascertained on his way to the village, I agreed, but had visions of our already large overdraft becoming vast if the problem with generator continued. How could we ever make the taverna pay?

"Jim, buy a new generator if you have to."

"No Liz, John and Angie will lend us theirs when they return, for at least two months, but we must get electricity soon."

"OK, I'll see what I can do. Bye for now, tell Ali to ring me next week as usual."

The Maddoxes were installed in the hotel, but not until Dixie and Annie had got them to bring buckets of sea water up as a store to flush the loos with. They went to the hotel to shower and ordered their last Martinis, with ice, Ali packed up all the food in the freezer again to give to Thanassis, "Having problems", he enquired.

"Oh not serious, just a minor hitch", Ali said through clenched teeth as she prepared to phone the Suzuki engineer and give him a blasting.

The remaining days for Dixie and Annie were spent with a self imposed schedule of water carrying, swimming, drinking, finding ingenious ways to overcome the lack of electricity and water, such as candlelit dinners with pasta cooked in salt water, and on their last night Dixie said, "You know Ali, what you should do is open up this place as an Endurance Centre, it has been so stimulating for us and we´ve lost weight." "Well, Dixie, that´s a great idea, but I work here to try and give people a perfect holiday - with no hassles, but on this island perhaps we should change our way of thinking... perhaps you´re right."

Car loaded

CHAPTER 9

THE ULYSESS VOYAGE

I sold my house in June, not at the sum I anticipated, but I had enough to stash away in an off shore account and what with the interest and my widow´s pension, I thought I would have enough to live on in Greece.

I paid back the loan to Simon, who had now found himself a small terraced house in London to use as a base. One room in it was allocated to me to store a few posessions and to use when I returned to England for my hospital check ups and Christmas.

It all happened so quickly, but when I came to dispose of my antique furniture which I had acquired over many years, I felt that I was losing a part of my life. Every item meant something to me, I could recall where and when I bought it and how the furniture had moved with me and to which spot in each room.

I had continued my psychotherapy in the form of psychodrama in a fortnightly group run by a brilliant director and a beautiful person called Jinnie Jefferies. Jinnie had become a personal friend and although we did not know it then, she was also to make her home in Greece. It was my last psychodrama session before I left for good and Jinnie cleverly brought out my fears and worries about leaving England.

In psychodrama you use the group to act your problems so that at the end of the enactment there is a catharsis which helps the protagonist see an answer or reason for their problems.

Every member of the group became a piece of my precious furniture! It sounds absurd, but it worked. I could say Good-Bye to my four poster bed, my grandfather clock, my Sheraton table, my Victorian chairs. I told them how much I had appreciated them and valued their aesthetic qualities, but realised that they would suffer if exposed to the Mediterranean sun, so I could then get rid of them. When the dealer came to take them away I wished them a happy new home, they would not have fitted into the house in Greece where most of one's life is spent outside. Not that the Greeks do not take a pride in their houses, the women spend a lot of the day sweeping and cleaning.

I remember a time when I was exploring a remote village and a peasant woman asked if I would like a coffee? We were in her courtyard and she shooed away the chickens and then took up her broom to sweep away their droppings, having satisfied herself I would not get my shoes dirty, she fetched a red plastic beer crate, which she inverted for me to sit on, then brought a large olive oil tin to use as a table. Simplicity and minimalism is what I would now aim for... But not without electricity!

I wrote to my Euro Labour M.P. telling her of the problems we were encountering with the electricity. Greece after all, was now in the Common Market. I pointed out that I had paid a large sum of money as a deposit, but that the DEH were still procrastinating and our business was suffering as a result. We were part of the tourist industry upon which Greece relies for a major part of its economy. I received a very civil letter back saying that she "Sympathised and had sent my letter on to the relevant department at the British Embassy in Athens who would intervene".

Ali had phoned to say they had John and Angie's generator again and they wouldn't buy a new one yet as they had bribed the man with the only digger on the island to start digging holes for the columns. He had coveted a fluffy parrot which we had hanging in the bar. It had a small tape recorder up its bottom and when anyone sat underneath it, the parrot would repeat the first six words of the sentence spoken.

The Digger man would come for a beer and sit and talk to the parrot, beaming with delight when he heard his voice played back. If we were lucky Ali said we might have electricity this month.

I needed a car in Greece to enable Ali to do the shopping for the Taverna and also because I wanted to travel within Greece and be independent. I found just what I wanted, a left-hand drive Fiat Panda, 1000 cc, I would have been at a disadvantage with a right-hand drive car with the erratic driving in Greece.

Arthur and I went up to Gloucester to inspect the car. It had been owned by a couple who had lived in France and bought the Panda there, but now they wanted a right-hand drive vehicle. There it stood, gleaming white, only thirty thousand kilometres on the clock, an AA certificate and recent service bills, the back seat went down allowing for bulky purchases - it was perfect.

"This is Ulysses", I told Arthur.

We had always named cars in our family, after my first purchase of a Morris Minor and the children had said it should be "Wee Willie Winkie".

"It's going to do a lot of voyages, inside and outside of Greece."

"That's a good idea", Arthur said.

"Yes isn't it."

"No not the name of the car... we could start a charter with "Arion Bleu" which would follow the route Ulysses took..."

"Arthur, we aren't even making any money with the present charter and Yacht Club let alone paying for more advertising for another scheme!"

I paid two thousand Pounds for Ulysses and before I left I had two sun roofs cut into the top and extravagantly bought a radio/cassette to keep me entertained on my travels.

We had booked the car on the ferry from Ramsgate to Dunkirk in mid June, Arthur planned the route meticulously, (he enjoyed this job as it made him think he was plotting a chart on "Arion Bleu"). We weren´t going to dawdle through Europe and planned on arriving at Ancona in Italy in two-and-a-half days. I had said good-bye to my social work colleagues and to my clients. I found the latter the most difficult. Many of them felt abandoned and angry, also resentful that I could start a life elsewhere without the depravations they were confronted with, but they gave a party and presented me with a huge bunch of flowers, an expensive pen and a large card inscribed by them all, with comments such as... "Good Luck you old bag", "Good Luck and good riddance mate", "Don´t forget us", and one particularly moving note..., "To the best social worker I have ever had - I will never have another!"
My tears flowed as I looked at their embarrassed faces and their children all dressed in party clothes, they had given me so much over the years, made me humble and aware of what a privileged person I was in comparison, I didn´t want to leave them, only the system which labelled single parents as "Inadequate spongers". Perhaps from my example they might come to realise that a single Mum can get away from the inevitable circumstances associated with their state and find a different future...
"We´ll be over to see you if we can get Gran to look after the kids", "Ta Ra", they hovered around the door waving and whistling and singing "For she´s a jolly good fellow!"
I couldn´t look back because I would have seen myself twenty years before.

I´ve never been good at saying good-bye. A Past Life Medium once told me that I had been a mercenary in a previous life. I must have been called to fight many times and rushed away to what could have been my death, I felt like this now, so I tried to be positive as I hugged and kissed Fiona and Simon as they stood with Arthur in the street beside Ulysses, now piled high. The luggage rack bearing my only antique item, an apothecaries chest with lots of drawers which I was sure would be useful in Greece. Fiona´s pert little face was screwed up into a cross between a smile and tears. She was feeling abandoned again - first her father - now her mother.

"Darling, you´re a big girl now! And you can come over for holidays with Steve."

"It´s not the same" she blurted out. "I can´t see you when I want to or ring and talk to you because you haven´t got a phone."

"But I´ll write and I´ll be back for Christmas."

Simon had arranged to come out in August for a month before he started University.

"Good journey Mum. Arthur take it easy... cool man."

As we drove away I saw him put a protective arm around his sister.

"They´ll be OK", Arthur reassured me as he glanced in the side mirrors to pull away (we couldn´t see out of the rear window because of luggage).

"Kids are resilient, anyway you´re not going to Timbuctoo."

I felt that I was, as the familiar English landscape of rolling fields and green deciduous trees receded from view. The driving through the flat countryside of Belgium, France and onto the never ending "Autobahn" in Germany, stopping only once for the night in Frieburg in a hotel which had designated "smoking" and "non smoking bedrooms". On through Switzerland´s towering mountains and the Mont Blanc tunnel until we arrived in Italy and the sunshine at last. We stuck to the motorways with the Ferraris leaving Ulysses behind in their trails of exhaust, until we reached Ancona for a night crossing.

Apart from my apothecaries chest inside the car I had bought a televison, radio and cassette player (as there was still a large electrical tax on imported electrical goods in Greece), and balanced on the top of the car were a rake and hoe I had purchased in England, because I had never seen these gardening implements in Greece, only pick axes and shovels. Arthur and I had stopped at an Italian delicatessen to stock up with many pungent Italian cheeses which we would not be able to buy either. These we wrapped in foil and put inside the car. Whilst we were waiting to board the ferry we got into conversation with a German couple on a motor bike, they were inspecting our load with interest.

"Are you Archaeologists?", the man asked.

"Gracious me, what gave you that idea?"

"*Vell you ave ze tools for excavating with you.*"

If he had come to this misinformed conclusion what would the Greek customs think? We did not want to be charged on entry for planning to take away their precious antiquities without a licence, so we scrabbled around for newspaper to cover the tools and thanked the Germans profusely.

After a smooth twenty-four hour crossing via Corfu, we arrived in Patras. There is nothing remarkable about the scenery when you enter from the sea into the port, but I was excited prior to that when about two miles west of Patras I saw the outline of the barren, conical mountain which towers above Messolongia, where our notorious countryman Lord Byron died during the fight for independence against the Turks. Byron is revered throughout Greece and there are statues, streets, hotels and squares named in his honour.

At the customs Arthur said "Don´t look suspicious."

"How can I change what I look like?"

"Well the only time I´ve ever been stopped at customs is when you are with me, just take off your sunglasses and smile."

An officious customs man came over to us, he demanded passports and car registration details, then peered inside the over laden Ulysses.

"Open", he commanded.

With visions of losing all my electrical goods I fumbled with the key and undid the boot - the customs man reeled back holding his nose,

"*Panagia mou*!" the Italian cheeses had strengthened during the crossing and the Gorgonzola and Dolce Latte were humming, sending out an odour which was certainly repellent to him. He waved us through the customs with a look of relief as I closed the boot.

With his foot on the accelerator Arthur sped through the dock gates into the anonymity of the seething mass of cars which jammed the streets in the rush hour.

"We made it! We´re on Greek soil now."

There was no going back and Ulysses was purring with delight as if he knew he had come home.

CHAPTER 10

IT MAKES FAWLTY TOWERS LOOK LIKE CLARIDGES...

The sight of Trizonia, with its now familiar three green hills rising from the tranquil blue sea and the feel of the warm sun on my face, dispelled any ambivalent feelings I had about leaving England.

We left Ulysses parked and still loaded (except for the cheese), on the mainland by the jetty and caught the water taxi across the straits.

Xristos proffered a hand "*Ti kaneis?* Welcome."

"We´re tired but well and a bit smelly", Arthur said as he held the cheese away from him.

"Xristos, I would like to go to the village first, then round to the house as I have to phone Fiona and Simon to tell them we´ve arrived safely."

"OK *Leez*, no problem."

The village hadn´t changed, there was no sign of activity, a couple of old men were seated in the taverna, clacking their worry beads and holding conversations with each other from separate tables. Babba Jannis waved a greeting from outside Spiros, and then as I walked to Thanassis´ mini-market, the old men, Kosta, Thanos and Babbis all rose to greet me, "Bravo *Kiria Leez.*"

This was unprecedented, to get up and shake hands with a "Foreign Lady", usually the greeting was a nod and a "*Yeia sou*", whether I´d been away for three months or a week. Then Papa Xristos came bustling out of the Taverna, grasping both my hands.

"Bravo Madam."

Yeia mas! - Three captains at table

Was it because I had driven through Europe in two-and-a-half days!

I phoned Simon and told him to tell Fiona we had arrived safely then went to pay for the call.

"Well done *Leez*, good to see you", Thanassis said as he put the money in the drawer, then Ileas and Aspassia appeared, kissing me on both cheeks and more "*Bravos*".

As I climbed back on to the boat I said to Xristos "What are all the 'Bravos' about, I've never had such a greeting here?"

"It's a secret", he grinned, "but you'll soon find out."

As we rounded the lighthouse into the second bay I noticed something different on the landscape, all along the road from the corner of the village where the bay curves round, there were electricity columns! The last one was in my garden and between each column there were cables, extending to the house!

"Arthur look - we've got real power, electricity at last!"

"Surprised eh?" Xristos smiled, "You know why everyone came to congratulate you in the village, because Ali told them you wrote to your MP and you beat the system without having to resort to backhanders. Everyone knows. Perhaps you'll be the next Mayor of Trizonia."

Alison was jumping about on the jetty, tanned and blonde, her unruly hair straining to escape the confines of her sun hat.

"Mum, Hi have you seen them? We've got electricity."

"When did the miracle happen?"

"Only two days ago after you left England. They dynamited the ground and did it all in two days. Oh, the bliss of being able to turn on a switch and knowing the lights will work. No more bloody generators, no more noise, it's unbelievable, clever Mum", she hugged me then turned to Arthur.

"Hi Arthur - give us a kiss, - poo! What is that smell, excuse me."

"This, Alison is our passport to freedom", he waved the cheese bag under her nose.

"I hope you´re going to eat it soon or else it will walk away."

In the evening, sitting in the warm breeze on the balcony with our lights now shining as brightly as those in the village, we exchanged news. Jim, we learnt, had rescued two kittens whose mother had been run over in Lepanto, and they were now living aboard the yacht, until the next charter.

"They´ll be good for keeping the mice down in the Taverna."

"Can´t stand cats", Ali and I said in unison. "Anyway we´ve got Kebab."

"You can´t have a Greek taverna without lots of cats - people expect them."

"Mickey how are you?"

"I´m fine Lizzie", and she looked glowing, but I noticed the look she gave Alison as though to say "Do I tell?"

"Well Mum we didn´t want to tell you on your first night..."

"Tell me - what? Not another drama with the house?"

"No, it´s just that... well", Mickey drew a deep breath. "I want to leave... but I don´t really."

"Sorry darlings, I don´t understand, please tell me clearly."

It turned out that Mickey had fallen in love with a Greek/ Canadian man who had sailed in on a yacht to Trizonia and stayed for two weeks, resulting in him offering Mickey the fare to Canada from England in two weeks time.

"You see he is everything I´ve been searching for years Liz, and he´s in the same graphics business and can give me work so I can eventually get my Green Card and go to New York", Mickey poured out her feelings. "I thought you wouldn´t mind helping Ali in the Taverna until she can get someone else, I can´t just leave her on her own, but I want to go with Tinos."

"Mickey if that´s important to you of course I´ll help", but I looked at Ali who was tight lipped and thought "I wonder if this is going to work?"

We loved each other very much but with her need for perfection and my laissez-faire attitude there could be difficulties.

"We'll discuss it tomorrow properly, but one thing - I really do not want to cook, serving is OK."

I had been cooking for a family all my life and I didn't intend becoming a cook for half the British Fleet now.

"I don't mind making a few crêpes suzettes or banana fritters", Arthur, who had a sweet tooth ventured.

"No way" Ali said, "there is not room for two chefs in my kitchen, you can help serve the drinks, but you're only here for two weeks so we've got to have a system for when you're not around."

Arthur ordered another Drambuie, "Only trying to help."

"Actually Arthur you could be of help about the lighting system", Jim said. "Now we've got power we have got to change the wiring as the voltage is too low."

"Tell me more", Arthur and Jim grouped together and bent their heads over paper and Arthur was engrossed in mathematical calculations immediately.

I went to bed in the living room, unaware of the clatter of dishes, voices of customers, the only sound I remember as I fell asleep was the trilling of the night cicadas.

Waking early I tip-toed onto the balcony to watch the huge yellow sun rising over the mountains, it was hot by nine a.m. There were about ten yachts at anchor in the bay below and not a breath of wind to ripple the surface of the sea, this amazing view would be there every morning of my life from now on.

Mickey's last week and my week's holiday went quickly, I met Angie and John who were still moored below us, their good nature and generosity captivated me and they were a permanent feature of the Taverna now.

One afternoon they took us all to the beach on the other side of the island for a barbecue. John could not get over the fact that the latest English man who was staying, went swimming in his pyjamas.

"Bloody pommies, what sort of behaviour is that, he'll get his bowler hat out next!"

"John, he's got a fair skin, that's why", whispered Angie as she turned the sizzling pork chops on the charcoal.

"Well why doesn't he stay in bed then?"

I brought my possessions over to the house, the apothecaries chest hung on the wall, crammed full of creams, lotions, soaps and first-aid supplies and homeopathic pills; the television and video looked out of place in my typically spartan Greek room. I hung my few pictures of England above the table, Sue had taken three different photos of the English countryside and mounted them together with the inscription "England", lest I forget. I placed my favourite photos of Fiona and Simon on the shelf, and the mosquito net hung over my bed, this kept the flies and wasps out as well as the irritating mosquitoes. The room was my space for the summer, I had to share the rest of the house with the guests and a constant stream of changing customers.

I was left in charge of the Taverna for the first time when Ali took Mickey to the village and then to catch the bus to Athens to join her beloved Tinos.

Ali had instructed me about the running of the Taverna. I was to ask customers if they wanted drinks first, serve them, then take the orders for food on a pad which had a copy, I had to number them in order of priority and Ali would stick them on nails above her preparation counter. I also had to stack the dishes afterwards into the ancient leaking dishwasher and was reminded that I should remain cheerful at all times.

The tables were polished, flowers in the centre, napkin holders, salt and pepper and toothpicks to one side, I had mopped the floor and propped the Visitors Book beside the door, the fairy and path lights were on. I was ready for opening at seven p.m. My only customers for the first hour were Arthur, Jim, John and Angie, they were drinking beers so I could manage them easily.

"Where's your pinafore and cap Liz?" joked Arthur as he looked at my skimpy shorts and flip-flops.

"It's bloody hot in the kitchen, I'm not wearing more than I have to", I retorted as I glanced at my watch, it was eight o'clock. Alison hadn't yet returned. I had chopped all the vegetables for salads and garnish, but I did not know where the main dishes were in the freezer, nor how to prepare them. Then a French couple arrived. I took their drinks order then gave them the menu, praying they would only have starters and salad.

"Here she is", Jim pointed over the balcony to Ali who was motoring over to the house with two other people in the "dory". She arrived at the door very red in the face.

"Darlings so sorry, but guess who I met on the way over - David and Claire." She introduced me to a lean, tanned attractive Canadian man and his very pretty and equally tanned Dutch girl friend.

"Yeah, we lured your daughter on board for an *ouzo*", drawled David, "but once Ali and the "Duchess" get together there's nothing holding'em, turned into quite a session!"

"Well she's here now", disarming me with her wide and beautiful smile, Claire took a seat outside.

"Yes, but in what state?" I thought as I heard Ali clattering about in the kitchen.

The French man and his wife were ready to order and I carefully wrote in my pad one *Tzatziki*, one Chili con Carne, two kebabs with baked potatoes. They ordered wine by the jug and I gave the order to Ali in the kitchen, she was fairly drunk but trying not to show it.

"Right here we go", she pinned the slip onto the nail and peered at it, "you do the *Tzatziki* and I´ll do the Chili con Carne."

I took the jug of cold wine out to the couple then prepared the bread basket and *Tzatziki*. I returned to the kitchen to find Ali standing by the gas burner with a jar of chili powder in her hand, which she was liberally sprinkling into the saucepan.

"Go easy on the chili", I cautioned.

"Oh shut up", she gracelessly replied.

I took the French people more bread as I could see they might die from hunger the way things were going in the kitchen, then went to attend to David and Claire´s orders, they had joined Arthur and the others.

There was a loud clanking of the ship´s bell from the kitchen, which meant the order was ready for the customers. I bore the steaming chili out to the customers.

"Merci, what a beautiful presentation, we´ve never ´ad anything like this in Greece."

"Thank you, Bon Appetit", I said obsequiously as I backed away.

I smelt the kebabs frying so knew Ali had succeeded in mastering the next dish, so sat with Arthur and company to sip a glass of wine and put my feet up.

"Liz, I think the French want you", Angie motioned with a tilt of her head.

I looked over to see the man waving at me from the other table. "Yes, can I get you something?"

He had his hand to his mouth and was scarlet in the face, "Water - please - water!"

"It is a very 'ot dish", his wife said, "I sink too 'ot for 'im".

"I am so sorry, but I did explain it was spicy when you ordered it. Can I get you something else instead?"

"Yes, please we will 'ave plain kebabs for two."

I whisked away the offending dish and rushed into the kitchen.

"Ali, you've been a little heavy handed with the chili, that man's on fire. Try some yourself!"

She dipped a spoon into the pan and tasted a minute amount, her face went crimson: "Help water quick!"

That sobered her up and after giving the order for another bland helping of kebab, I took a large jug of water to the long suffering Frenchman and a complimentary jug of wine.

"With apologies from the chef."

David and Claire who had heard the drama were grinning, as were the others, I went to take their orders.

"I'm afraid the Chili con Carne is not on the menu tonight, but we have everything else, what will it be?"

There were many other incidents which precluded us from reaching the five star Michelin Category, but Alison struggled on valiantly learning to eliminate those dishes which couldn't be frozen or kept easily in the heat of the summer.

I wasn't a trained waitress and although I tried to please, I treated the customers as they treated me. If they were raucous and rowdy with a tendency to banter and jokes, I would laugh with them or tell them to behave, they didn't mind; the quiet and romantic couples holding hands and gazing at the moon as it rose behind the mountain, I would interrupt only to give them their food.

The romantic atmosphere was difficult to achieve after we

Alison cooking

had an outbreak of mice and rats in the ceiling. We had put rat poison down, which we were assured would send them racing out of house to find water. It didn´t work like that. Some of them died in the area just above the entrance to the Taverna, where we could not remove them. The smell was disgusting, we sprayed the area with Fresh Air spray, Lavender water and even Guerlain but to no avail, I ended up by pouncing on customers and dragging them round to the balcony before they reached the smelly zone.

Despite the chaos and mistakes we had many customers and yachts people who became our friends and returned later in the season. I always offered the "Visitors book" at the end of a meal so that we could gauge the general feeling about the time the customers had spent with us. Some of the inscriptions were very complimentary (admittedly many in a drunken hand).

But the classic remark was entered later in the season when we had a particularly hectic night, with customers having to sit on the steps because there were not enough tables, it read "Enjoyed the view and food, This place makes Fawlty Towers look like Claridges!"

Greek house split in half

CHAPTER 11

GETTING TO KNOW THE GREEKS

In the daytime when we were not working we would often go to the village, either to collect the post before it blew away or for lunch or a mezzes.

The villagers were becoming more accepting of us and as my Greek improved I was able to sit and chat, at a basic level still. They would ask... "How's it going up there?" as though we lived ten miles away rather than eight hundred metres. Most of them, because they were elderly, never left the village except to tend their goats or gather brushwood.

The oldest man on the island was Kosta, he was very proud of his eighty-nine years and I would walk with him slowly to the corner of the road beside the sea. He wore a big straw hat and leaned heavily on his stick, but his mind was sharp and he would reminisce on the way.

No one had lived on Trizonia until about two hundred years ago, their families all lived in the mountain village opposite, but then as the danger from marauding pirates and the Turks receded they came to live beside the sea. Trizonia had no water then and they would have to row across to the mainland everyday for their supplies. They planted olives and vines, built houses and a small church and lived off the land or from fishing. Each islander had his own *caique* as the only way to leave the island in the past had been a big *caique* which would stop off and then visit other ports along the coast. There was no main road then and life was very hard. "Did you know Onassis wanted to buy this island?" Kosta said.

"No, really."

"Yes, he offered us all money to leave Trizonia but we refused to go, why should we move when we had our vines and land, no amount of money could take that from us."

Gradually children were born and a school house built on the slopes beside the church, but it became apparent that there were not enough jobs or work on the island to supply everyone with a livelihood, and the young people were tempted by the life in the big cities, Athens, Thessaloniki and Patras could provide them with the comforts of modern technology which could not be found on Trizonia. So there was an exodus of most of the young men - not the women, at that time they were still expected to stay at home.

The older women were inquisitive (a Greek characteristic) and would invite me into their well-kept houses for a coffee and delicious sweet cakes which they had prepared themselves.

Their living quarters consisted of one room with a large fireplace, a table, bed and gas burner, and a black and white television in a prominent position, usually covered with a crocheted cloth. In the outhouse their store of olive oil and wine was kept in barrels for use during the year, and whenever there was an abundance of fruit in season they would laden me with lemons, figs, pomegranates. They all had a plot to grow their own vegetables because they never knew when they would be cut off from the mainland by the strong winds which whipped the channel into a frenzied white froth. Faded family photos hung on the walls, the men in formal poses and usually in seamen´s uniform.

The conversation was predictable.

"Have you got a husband?"

When I replied "No, I am a widow", they would give me ill-concealed looks of disapproval when they saw I was not wearing black.

"How many children? Boys or Girls? How old are they?"

To have a large family ensured that you would be well cared for in your old age. Most of the women were content with their lives and although insular they were aware of politics worldwide since the advent of television, but the gossip in the village was more interesting than any "COUP" in Africa. It was comforting to walk to the village and to see the same faces and be greeted with "How are you?" One always replied in the affirmative "Well, thank you".

One day when Alison had a sore throat she replied, "Not well thanks, I´m feeling terrible".

The enquirer looked surprised and said, "Why did she say that?"

Jim found their constant inquisitiveness annoying, at every encounter they would say "*Pou Pas* (Where are you going)?" he wanted to say "Mind your own business", but apparently there is no such expression in Greek.

I learned that all the locals had nick names to enable them to differentiate between the thirty Kostas, Yiorgos and Nicos who lived in the village. (The grandfather´s name is handed down to the first son.)

There was a man of about seventy, with blue eyes and a crinkled weather beaten face who walked with bow legs, Yiorgo was nick named "The look out man", because he lived in a house at the end of the promontory overlooking the mainland and the sea. They thought that the unusual colour of his eyes (for that region) meant he had clearer vision.

When I saw him he would ask me if I was going to Lepanto to do my shopping and could he have a lift. He wouldn´t go when it was too hot, raining or too early, but one day the

Two greek ladies in black

Gods were favouring him and we drove together. I parked "Ulysses" beside the sea front and Yiorgo walked to the beach and peed in the sea, then came back to me doing up his flies. There were other people lying on the beach but they paid no attention and I noticed afterwards how commonplace it was for Greek men to relieve themselves whereever they were. I wished women could urinate with such aplomb.

Yiorgo wanted some seeds so I followed him to a cobbled street near the harbour where there was an old shop. Outside hung goat and sheeps bells, shepherds crooks, and a variety of herbs. Inside there were large boxes of seeds which the shop owner would weigh on his old fashioned brass scales. I bought a half a kilogram of camomile, it seemed like a vast amount until I started to strip the flowers from the stalks and was left with one small bag to make into tea.

On the water taxi back to the island Yiorgo said "Thank you *Leez*."

"Will you be my guest at the festival on the fifteenth of August?"

"What festival Yiorgo."

"The most important festival after Easter... *Panagia*. That is the day when all those who are very ill travel to the Monastery on Tinos, where the Icon of Our Lady was found. They hope for a miracle to cure them, everywhere in Greece we celebrate this special day."

"Thank you Yiorgo, if we are not busy I will come."

We decided to close the Taverna and Ali and I joined Yiorgo and his sister, Anita, on the mainland then drove up the hair pin bends to the small village of Ileas. In the square the tables were set out under the huge plane tree, at one end of the square a platform had been made for the musicians, the Clarino player, (a man with the biggest hands I had ever seen), produced a

Tin can car

pure mellow tone from this traditionally Greek instrument, two *Bouzouki* players, an accordianist and a female singer, dressed in a diamante encrusted black dress, were warming up.

There were amplifiers hanging in the trees and micro-phones were emitting shrill squeaks, as we sat ourselves down at a long table, to be joined by Iota, her husband Takkis and their four beautiful wide-eyed children.

The village oven was piled with charcoal on which whole lambs were roasting. Pieces of the meat were cut off and placed on the table in a paper tablecloth - salad, bread and beer and wine were brought to us and with our paper cups filled we toasted each other "*Yeia mas*, to your health, another good year and a good winter". No one noticed that I hadn´t eaten the lamb as they were all watching the musicians performing.

The noise was deafening, all the amplifiers were turned on full and conversation was impossible, Ali and I resorted to writing each other notes if we wanted to communicate. Then after more wine the assembled villages and guests found their "*Kefi*" (a word frequently used to express being in a happy mood) and the dancing started. Ali and I joined the circle trying to imitate the intricate steps which the children and adults performed expertly. Then exhausted we collapsed at the table, but the Greeks went on late into the night and long after we had left we could still hear the music on the island ten kilometres away. I asked Yiorgo on the way back why they had the music so loud?

"So that people in other villages who have not got musicians can here the music and enjoy it too", he said. "Some of the villages are very remote and the band can´t get to them all in one evening!"

Sailor mending net

CHAPTER 12

SAILORS´YARNS

In September the sun lost its intensity and the mornings and evenings were cooler but the sea still warm. The beautiful view around Trizonia became more clearly defined without the heat haze and the silhouette of the mountains showed up in detail against the blue of the sky. I felt a rise in my energy level, and now I slept with a sheet over me, and could dispense with the whirring fan at night.

That month we had fewer paying house guests, there had been a steady stream of them since June, most had been obliging and easy going people but it was still a strain to be available for the constant queries, "How do you get to...? When is the bus? Can you order me a taxi".
I was happy when Martina and Simon arrived for their holidays and I could relax with familiar guests. Simon had brought his friend George, an eccentric boy of sixteen who was a doctor´s son. He was a complete hypochondriac owing to the fact that his father when training, would wake George at regular intervals during the evening to take his blood pressure. He brought a month´s supply of medicines with him and was wearing contrasting blue and green contact lenses when I met them off the ferry.
"Oh my God! What will the villagers think!" I wondered as George took off his hat to show his spiked green and red hair. We loaded their rucksacks on to the roof of the car, Martina chattering about her experiences on the plane with some Russian she had met.
"Babes it´s great to be here again, I´m longing to see Trizonia

and just relax, I've been working like a maniac and finished my last book so have no time schedule, Bliss oh bliss", she started stripping off her jumper and poked her feet out of the window of the car. "Mmm, fresh air!"

Simon told me about the results of his first years exams, which were excellent and about the friendships he had formed at University and I was so proud to know he had achieved the good results on his own, and that my absence had made no difference.

"Darling I hope you told George that there aren't any discos on Trizonia", I said when we were together.

"Mum don't worry, just because he looks trendy it doesn't mean he actually is, he's quite happy to sit in the sun."

"But not too much", I mused as I noticed George's transparently white skin.

Martina and I spent our days on the beach, swimming, reading and talking.

"I love your letters Lizzie, I can just visualise what's happening here, have you every thought of writing a book?"

"Yes often, but that's as far as it's got - thinking."

"Why don't you try now?"

"Look Mart, I'm still waitressing at night and helping Ali, when I have any free time all I want to do is swim and relax, my mind doesn't function too well in the heat."

"Yeah, but what about the winter time." Martina dived into the sea with nothing on and yelled, "Come on, in it's glorious."

But I sat under the parasol thinking about what she had said. Was there a story in the life I had chosen? For me it had seemed the right choice, a way to recover from cancer and an opportunity for self-discovery in an idyllic atmosphere. Was that material enough for a book? I'd think about it...

Evenings were busy now, the yachts were making for their winter destinations before the bad weather arrived in October, and night after night we would be serving the crews, Martina, Simon and George would sit with them.

John and Angie had, at last, left two months ago to finish their trip round the world with promises to keep in touch via other "Yachties" on their CB network.

Martina could not believe it when a retired English couple and the owner of an old "Motor-sailor" told her they had taken only six weeks of sailing lessons before they left England and only knew how to set the sails in a certain direction, so could never plan a particular destination. They had no Admiralty charts either, just road maps of the coast line so they had to stay within sight of land!

Then there was the bearded, unassuming, sixty-year old lone sailor who would come up and sit quietly over a beer. Martina asked him which was his yacht, he pointed to a thirty-two foot sloop with self-steering attachment at the stern.

"Oh very nice, I suppose if you´re on your own it´s easier to handle a smaller boat, but I´d be quite nervous", she then went on to recount her journey in a larger boat when sailing to Brittany and in the Mediterranean, "Where have you sailed?" she asked.

"Around the world twice", he quietly replied. Martina choked on her wine and fixed him with a disbelieving stare, "In that!"

"Yes, I built her myself and she has always carried me safely, she is my perfect partner."

Simon and George were spell bound by this quiet man´s account of his experiences, and although he under played the history of his voyages, before he left Trizonia, he gave us a copy of his book. After reading it I realised what incredible fortitude and determination he had and reminded myself never again to judge a person by their outward appearance.

"I´m never going to talk about my sailing experiences again",
Martina stated.

There were the complete contrasts to the lone sailor, huge
motor launches flying the Royal Blue flags denoting affiliation
to the smartest yacht clubs in England. The owners would be
ferried to the jetty by the crew, immaculately dressed in white,
then they would spend the evening over dinner, on their ship
- to shore telephone, issuing instructions to the launch below,
never once looking at the spectacular view, the silver sliver
of a new moon or the star laden sky.

Then there were the sailing bores, the "Easterlies" and "West-
erlies" we called them, they would talk about sailing until
you could see their companions´s eyes glazing over.

"We had a jolly good beat into a westerly today, flew up
from Corinth, force seven, reefed in the main..." and on and
on.

Still it was a yacht club, I reminded myself as I picked up the
two hundred drachmas tip from a rich client who had bought
his own bottle of "Chateau Neuf du Pape".

"Hope you don´t mind, but Greek wines are rather rough."

"Yes we do mind", said Ali. "Charge him five hundred
drachmas corkage!"

The delivery crews of the gin palaces were very different
characters. One evening a ninety foot motor yacht dropped
anchor to the left of the yacht club and within five minutes
three large Dutch men arrived at the Taverna. They drank
vast quantities of beer and ordered a meal; because it had
rained that day and there was a fresh westerly wind we had
brought the tables inside. After finishing his meal the skipper
got up to check the boat from the balcony -

"Its gone!" he exclaimed, the other two leaped to their feet to join him, as we did; the blaze of light which had marked the position of the ninety footer was nowhere to be seen. They peered at the shore below us with the desperate hope that she might be tucked down on the beach... nothing.

"Let´s go", they raced down the steps and sped off in their tender out of the bay.

They moored in a place sheltered from the west wind then came back up to the Taverna. Only two of them, the other Dutchman was left on watch.

"She had run aground on the island opposite, no real damage, she´a pile of shit anyway, even the compass doesn't work and we´re meant to be taking her to Turkey. The owner won´t maintain her, he just comes to join us when we´re in port to show his wealthy friends, stays one night and leaves. Never mind, I´ve brought some of his champagne up to celebrate the salvaging, won´t you join us?"

My favourite character was the Russian Professor of Physics, who had planned a journey from the Black Sea, via the Mediterranean, through to the Bay of Biscay returning via the Baltic to St.Petersburg on a windsurfer!

He had his suitcases strapped on to the board, and when the board went into the water so did his belongings. He had to stay close to the shore, but had one stretch of eleven hours near the coast of Greece; he sang as he sailed and knew full opera scores, and he sang the music of "My Fair Lady" while we accompanied him on guitar with the words in English, before we gave him a bed for the night. He slept for fifteen hours.

Before Simon and George left we promised them a night out off the island at a Bozouki. Ali, Martina and I dressed in party gear went by "dory" to the village where we were met by Xristos to take us to the mainland.

"All aboard", Xristos proffered his hand as we jumped from the harbour wall. "Ladies last." SPLASH...

"Help, Help!"

"I can´t believe it - it´s not Mart? She´s done it again. How can anyone fall in through such a tiny gap."

"Well she´s not very big."

"Don´t let her hear you say that", I said as we fished Mart out, with her finery now soaking wet and with strands of seaweed in her freshly washed hair. Xristos produced a towel and she rubbed herself vigorously.

"I suppose we had better take you back to change!"

"No way, I´ll go as I am, I´ll soon dry out dancing", Martina who is normally a careful and neat dresser had become affected by the spontaneity and magic of Greece.

"Go for it Xristos, start the engine, *Bozouki* here we come!"

Arthur came back to Trizonia the week after the boys had left. He said he had returned to help us with the flotillas.

In the kitchen he sploshed water over the floor, cigarette ash into the rinsing water and wheezed his way round the tables offering liqueurs to the lead members of the crews. He encouraged the Australian lead crews to join in the game of "Black Spot", where each participant has to say the same phrase and if they make a mistake they are marked with the end of a charred cork, each further mistake results in more spots and the first to receive ten spots is the loser.

"Thank God the season is ending, I couldn´t go on like this", I said as I slouched at the table, my face covered with black spots which had run into a big black blob.

"I think you´ve done very well for the first season, a few more nights like this and we will have cleared our overdraft."

"Arthur, I like your optimism but you havn´t been here all year", Ali pointed out.

"It´s not just the food and service you saw tonight, it´s the logistics of running this place which are very difficult, and some people have not enjoyed the haphazard way, so will they come again?"

"Ali, it seems the majority have enjoyed themselves," I flipped through the Visitors Book. "There are many compliments about your cooking."

"They were all drunk", but she smiled and I knew she was proud of her achievements which the book had ratified.

"However, I think Ali is right and we do need to look at the economics of this venture", I said. "At the moment Ali takes the money for meals and bar, and for the rooms; but I know Ali has to clean and service the rooms and change and wash the linen, that takes time from her work in the Taverna leaving her working for nothing."

"OK, I´ll work out the finances tomorrow so we can have a plan for the future." Arthur wished us "Good night" then groped his way down the steps to the boat.

In the late morning we studied his sums. It appeared that from the letting of the rooms (if occupied by the same amount of people as this year), we could just survive without increasing our overdraft. But it meant continuing to be economical with our living standards and having to find the cheapest charter flights whenever we travelled.

Arthur suggested that now we had electricity, we could provide "Yachties" with a shower and washing machine facilities, charging for the usage, and that would help pay for the bills.

He thought Jim might be able to design and build a trolley, run with a winch, beside the steps, to make the job of having to bring crates and shopping up to the Taverna easier. The latter idea was more for his benefit than anybody else´s, because of his struggle with the steps!

"Perhaps we could also open a Sailing and Windsurfing School and give tuition in Water Skiing?"

"Why don´t we buy some donkeys and provide Donkey Trekking round the island while we´re about it?" I facetiously remarked.

"And who´s going to buy the donkeys and look after them when the house is closed? Lizzie, will you be practical - just because you want their manure for your garden! Anyway, if my suggestions were implemented these new facilities should improve our incomings. We will probably never make any money out of this crazy venture, but we don´t want to lose any more. It´s a way of life more than a business - I don´t suppose anyone will ever make a´take over bid´nor that we will have to "Go Public"!"

"Bravo Arthur, good ideas, and we can start in the spring when the weather is better."

We jointly agreed that these plans should be carried out next year. But the end of the season brought work of a different kind.

The "dory" had to be lifted from the water, the engine serviced, the lasers stowed and sails washed. Jim and Arthur then prepared "Arion Bleu" for her journey to Malta where she was to be taken out of the water during the winter.

Ali and I had to visit the Tax Office and return her licence to the Police informing them of our closure over the winter months. Stock taking was completed and fridge and freezers emptied and the whole house cleaned.

But on my birthday in mid October we found time to go to the beach with a picnic. It was the first time I had swum on my birthday, the sea was warm and we had the beach to ourselves, the Greeks rarely went in swimming after the first of September. We gazed at the horizon where the sky was

150

becoming tinged with orange as the evening approached.

"I love this place", Ali said as we gathered up our towels.

"I think we've chosen well this time; I've enjoyed this crazy summer, but I'm going to miss you in the winter, I'm so used to the house being full of people and the noise and laughter. I'm a bit scared."

"Are you afraid of being alone?"

"No, not alone in the context of company, but alone with my thoughts, no distractions to prevent me looking inside myself, I'm afraid of what I might discover."

"That's one of the reasons you came here Mum, remember?"

Liz on beach

CHAPTER 13

WINTER ALONE

I returned to Greece on the fourth of January, having spent Christmas and New Year in England with my precious children and my friends. I was excited and yet wary at the thought of being on my own as I had never been alone for longer than two weeks in another country. I planned to use these next months constructively. To study and improve my Greek, to spend time on self-healing, analysis and meditation, and of course, preparing my vegetable garden and painting the house.

From the moment I landed at Athens Airport and was met by Ileas, our local taxi driver, I realised that in this country nothing could be planned. I had ordered a taxi, rather than taking the bus, because I wanted to be in Trizonia whilst it was still light. I had brought a load of books with me, so my luggage was heavy.

Ileas set off, as I thought, for Trizonia. But he explained, en route, that his mother had been ill, so he had to visit her in the hospital in Athens. We stopped to buy some flowers, then he disappeared, leaving me in the car for an hour.

"OK. *Leez*, now we go", he said on his return.

We then drove to the suburbs of Athens where he delivered, to a friend, some rather tired looking horta (greens from his land) and eggs from his own chickens.

The crazy speed and wild disorder of the city traffic made me feel rather sick and I longed to be in Trizonia. I had now been travelling for five hours and I knew it would take another three hours to get there.

Eventually we were on our way, driving through landscape dominated by vines and fruit trees, interspersed with acres of already cropped cotton, through the middle of a wide plain where most of the cotton produce of Greece comes from.

I forgave him the delay when we arrived over the mountains to see the vivid blue sea once again. The road, now hugging the coast, cut into massive lumps of rock which rose steeply from the sea to snow-capped peaks. Then, quite suddenly, there was my island, nestling close to the mainland.

Ileas stopped at the shop while I bought a few provisions for the nightbread, cheese and milk. I got out with my luggage onto the jetty. There were no water taxis in sight. Ileas explained that Xristos, my friendly water taxi man, was in Athens and that Captain Yannis' boat was out of the water for the winter.

"What about Nico's boat?" I asked.

"*Ela*, that's another story", he said.

"What do you mean?"

"*Poli provlima*", he said, then explained why Nico's boat was out of action. It appears that one night two men who were working on the dredger at the marina had got drunk. They decided to have a joy ride and taken Nico's boat round and round the island at top speed until the engine blew up!

"So, how do I get to the island?", I enquired.

"*Oxi provlima*", Ileas reassuringly said.

He went to the phone and returned beaming.

"Kosta, the Mayor, will come and collect you", he said.

We drank a coffee together, and another and another, until I saw an unfamiliar boat crashing through the large waves towards us. It was indeed the Mayor, but with the tug boat which was being used to pull the crane for the new marina. With a wide smile and "*Yeia Sou's*", Kosta piled my luggage onto the deck of the tug and we ploughed our way across the

154

channel separating the island from the mainland.

It was now six o'clock. The locals were sitting inside the tavernas, I couldn't get my cases round to the bay below the house because there was no boat man that would take me in this weather. So I left them in Spiros' taverna, took out what I needed for the night, and called on Aspassia and Ileas.

My friends were happy to see me back and insisted I have a drink and some mezzes. I gave them the presents I had bought them for Christmas - a small radio for Ileas and a jumper for Aspassia. She then plied me with food which she had prepared that day. Butter beans in tomato sauce, sardines which Ileas had caught that morning, fetta cheese and some of their own *Retsina* wine in a Coca-Cola bottle. It was getting dark, so promising to see them tomorrow I said "good-bye" and walked round the bay to my house.

When I reached the bottom of the steps I heard a plaintive miaowing. Jim's cats, Benson and Sapho arrived to meet me. They were thin, but still alive, after two weeks of fending for themselves. I put my bag down on the path while I lifted up the barrier of twigs and brushwood. Ileas had placed this at the opening to deter any strangers from coming up to the house in my absence.

The next moment I saw Sapho and Benson tearing at the bread and sardines in my plastic bag and then carrying them off, in their teeth, devouring my evening meal. I cursed them and they growled at me. I could not begrudge them their meal. They were, after all, just looking after themselves and I still had the butter beans and fetta. There was no sign of Kebab. I wondered if she had finally died.

It was now very cold as the sun had set. I opened the doors of my house.

"Hello, *spiti mou*", I said.

It smelt musty and damp. I switched on the lights... they worked!

and went into the kitchen. There were mice droppings all over the sink and claw marks on the soap. I went upstairs and made up my bed then ate what remained of the food Aspassia had given me. I drank the home-made *Retsina* and decided I was too tired to light the fire and would go straight to bed. I fetched the hot water bottle, which was a legacy from the previous owners, filled it and placed it in my bed, then quickly changed into my BHS winceyette pyjamas. It was too cold to wash, so I cleaned my teeth (the sign of a well brought up Middle Class English Person) and climbed into bed.

To my horror, the warm patch was also very wet! The Hotty Botty had leaked. The bed was soaking. Shivering, I turned the mattress, changed the sheets, then went downstairs to put on the kettle again. Behind the bar I found an empty *ouzo* bottle, I filled it with the nearly boiling water and trudged upstairs, but could hardly hold it as it was too hot, so I found a large thick sock, and placed the *ouzo* hot water bottle inside. Clutching this, I climbed into bed again. I felt warm and rather pleased with my new invention and as the waves of sleep enveloped me, I remembered wondering what problems tomorrow might bring.

I awoke to see the sun streaming through my bedroom window and blue skies. I jumped out of bed - then rapidly jumped back in again. It was still freezing!

I groped for my socks, thermal pants and vest from my drawer, rushed to find trousers and pullovers and some old woollen tights which I put on my head, and wrapped another pair around my neck. So this is the Mediterranean, I thought, as I lit both gas burners, one for warmth and one to prepare a cup of tea. Afterwards, thawing out a little, I managed to collect my thoughts. I knew I had to get food for a week as the journey to the nearest town was not simple. I would have to walk eight

Liz in "thermal wear"

hundred metres to the village along the dirt track road, then get a water taxi to the mainland. Then, providing my car was still there, drive for half an hour to the nearest town. I knew on these weekly expeditions there would be a lot to carry, so whilst in England I had brought one of those shopping bags on wheels, which are often used by the elderly, and cause severe damage to the legs and ankles when encountered in the supermarkets. I wouldn't be seen dead with one in England, but this was Greece and it was the only practical solution.

I set off down the thirty-five steps, ignoring the cats who were crying for more food, bumping my shopping trolley behind me.

On the way I noticed the houses were shuttered and there was no one to be seen. The population in winter had dwindled to eighty, the majority being men over fifty-five years old and a few women of the same age. There were only three men under forty, and the Mayor and his wife with three young children. A fourth was on the way.

"In order that the family can claim tax concessions", the Mayor blithely informed me!

As I wandered into the square I noticed that the fir tree in the centre was still bedecked for Christmas. Bits of tinsel fluttered from the branches, lanterns and coloured baubles were still dangling from the tree. They remained there until March!

I knocked on the door of Aspassia and Ileas' outhouse. They used this one room for living in during the winter. It had a large stone fireplace, or tsaki, which was large enough to burn huge olive trunks, and was alight day and night. Behind a floral curtain stood barrels of their own wine and olive oil. There was a stove, a canister of gas, a burner, a table and two chairs, a bed by the fire and a fridge with a large black and white television on top. It was simple, but warm and cosy.

Aspassia and Ileas like two children were curled up in bed together for warmth, fully clothed. Aspassia was dressed totally in black as a sign of respect for her mother, who had died the previous year. They greeted me, then Aspassia and I set off on the tug boat for shopping on the mainland.

I took the tarpaulin off my car which had been parked near the jetty since I left in early December. It went first time. Aspassia crossed herself, but refused to put on her seat belt. Not being Greek Orthodox and because it is now law in Greece, I strapped myself in.

I drove along the main road parallel to the sea, through orchards of orange and lemon groves, vivid dots of colour against the dark green leaves. Everywhere was so verdant, the colours in winter are such a contrast to the scorched arid landscape of summertime. I kept a look out for the flocks of sheep and goats which stray across the main road bringing all traffic to a halt. When this happens, the shepherd chats to the first driver in the queue, then saunters off waving his carved crook.

The nearest town, Lepanto, is well served with fruit and vegetable shops, hardware shops and supermarkets. There are also three banks and I could get all I needed there.

Leaving Aspassia to do her shopping, I set off with my trolley, which Aspassia coveted, and which caused consternation amongst other women shoppers.

"*Ti einai afto*?" Where can I find one?

I told them that I had bought it in England. This would lead to lengthy discussions about travel, politics, Margaret Thatcher and what was I doing in Greece this winter? It appeared that no English stay on a small island in the winter time, particularly not a woman "*moni sou!*" (alone).

It took me a long time to complete my shopping. I also had various tradespeople to see. Firstly, I needed to talk to Kosta, my plumber. He was seated behind his desk which was littered with papers, brimming ashtrays, and several empty coffee cups.

He got up, all four foot eleven of him. "*Xronia Polla. Kalo Himona*" (a greeting always given in New Year).

"*Leez*, it is cold, have drink to warm you."

Kosta then produced a Sprite bottle and poured me a glass.

"Thank you Kosta, but I don´t like Sprite", I said.

"This is no Sprite, this is my own Raki, from mountains. Especially we drink in winter to keep warm. I am beautiful!"

I never dared correct his constant misuse of English, because he tried so hard to impress me with his knowledge; anyway, it always made me laugh, because he was anything but beautiful. However, his mammoth personality compensated for his physical lack.

"*Yeia mas.*"

We clinked glasses and I swallowed the innocuous looking substance in one - following Kosta´s example. Pow! I thought I was going to rocket through the roof! This Raki was like fire water. It certainly warmed me, but I managed to avoid having any more by saying that I had to go to the bank. I asked Kosta to come over to my house to look at the water pump which was not working properly. We agreed on a set day. Then as I left, he walked after me, locking the shop door, and accompanied me to the bank.

The bank, as usual, had a long queue. Kosta paraded around saying "*Yeia sou´s*" to everyone, they all knew him. The bank was thick with cigarette smoke despite signs up saying "NO SMOKING" and "SMOKING IS BAD FOR THE HEALTH". The bank manager himself was a chain smoker and the staff

Kosta "I am beautiful"

followed his example. I needed to see Yannis, who was an English-speaking official, who had spent six months in Crawley, of all places!

"To improve my English", Yannis had told me.

"It is very beautiful in Crawley, but not like Greece."

How right he was. I asked Yannis to show me my statement and to explain how much I had in my account, Kosta followed me. He leant over the desk when Yannis produced the figures, then asked him how much I had and how much interest I would be getting. I realised that there is positively no confidentiality in Greek banks. They will openly discuss other people's financial situations and relish the details, particularly if in debt.

I left the bank with both Kosta and Yannis, still pouring over my account details, and made my way along the narrow pavements to the electrician's shop. I found Takkis, the owner, a large, gentle, middle-aged man with several other men huddled round his desk, staring at X-ray plates which Takkis was holding aloft.

"*Leez, xronia pola*", Takkis said.

I exchanged the greeting and asked him what was the interest in the X-rays.

"*Ela*- look at my leg", Takkis said.

He hauled himself up from his chair with the aid of a crutch and showed me a plaster cast encasing the whole of his right foot and leg. Apparently, he had been gardening with a sharp spade and had inadvertently driven the spade into his foot rather than the soil! I listened to all the gory details, interjecting with "*Ti cremas*" realising I could not possibly ask him now to come to the island to sort out my television aerial. I asked for a light bulb instead. He had installed my aerial in the autumn, proudly announcing, "Now you have colour *Leez*." But I never did!

Takkis' shop was like an Aladdin's cave of electrical components. They were lying everywhere in total confusion, from floor to ceiling, but he always knew where the tiniest part was kept. He couldn't reach the light bulb as it was on a top shelf, only accessible by rickety step ladders.

"You wait and have a drink with me, then I get my niece to go up the ladder." He ordered a coffee from the next door *kafenion*, which was brought on a circular metal tray with a central handle and a covering lid, designed specifically for the purpose, it is a common practice in Greece, if you do not have coffee-making facilities on the premises. Takkis produced a Pepsi cola bottle and poured a large *Raki* into my coffee cup.

"It is cold, *Leez*, this is good for you."

I knew what to expect his time, so let the warm liquid trickle down my throat and by the time his niece had found the bulb, I was feeling very mellow. I wove my way to the square to meet Aspassia, my basket brimming with goodies which I hoped would last me a week. I didn't dare to stop at any other shop for fear of offending another Greek if I turned down his home made *Raki*.

Back on Trizonia I lunched with Aspassia and Ileas on home made *tiropita* (cheese pie), a spinach and rice mixture, fetta and home-made *Retsina*. I was, by now, slightly drunk and incapable of carrying my suitcases and my shopping basket back to the house. The ever-obliging Ileas said he would bring them round for me in his boat. We piled everything into his small blue *caique*, called "Efi" after his daughter, and chugged across the inner bay to below my house. Ileas helped me load the goods onto the mechanised trolley Jim had so cleverly designed in order to avoid lugging heavy goods up the steep incline, and I zig-zagged up the steps, no longer feeling the cold.

The day after that I woke up with a headache. I staggered downstairs and peered out of the window, over the balcony and across the bay to the mainland. There was snow on Mud Mountain! Oh no! The locals had told me it hadn´t snowed here for fifty years. I was alone with no central heating, only a small wood-burning fire. I put on a woolly hat, gloves, two jumpers and trousers and boots and ventured into the garden. The snow clouds were swirling around the mountains opposite, there was ice on the water butt. I needed wood quickly. I started trying to cut up dead wood with an axe I had brought from England. It was blunt and made no impression on the bark. So I searched around in the shed and found an old saw. It took me an hour to cut through one branch. I was getting desperate, so I pruned as many small dead branches as I could reach, tiny brittle things which would not last any length of time. Then I trudged to the sea shore, with my Boss Bag and filled it with bits of driftwood which I thought might fit into the small aperture of my stove. As I was lugging the wood back, Ileas rode by on his donkey, Panagia.

"*Yeia sou Leez. Ti kaneis*?"

I told him about my problem and the lack of s uitable tools to cut wood.

"I will bring you some fuel", he said. "Don´t worry."

I deposited all the wood I had collected inside the house, working so hard I forgot about the cold. I gathered more small logs from the garden and dragged them into the shed. Then my saviour Ileas arrived with Panagia, up the steps, laden with wood.

He proceeded to cut it into the correct size for my stove, with a curved machete type implement, until there was a large heap of firewood. He then explained that I must start the fire with the roots of vines, as they burn easily. He pointed to the gnarled roots he had brought.

Inside the house I offered him an *ouzo*; whilst he drank this we discussed the weather and snow. Ileas felt it was going to get worse and advised me to get more wood. He agreed to chop down all my dead trees and cut them up for me. But he would not give me a price. I knew he was on a pension and trying to supplement the income of his son who was in the army. So I said that in return perhaps he would like to graze his goats and donkey on my land, and to cut any grass he needed for fodder. We shook hands on this, Ileas promising to come back when he had time. He had his own work to do, too.

The sky was darkening and I shut the doors and windows and went to light the fire. I took the metal top off, put in the paper and twigs, then once the vines had caught light, placed my precious logs upon them. The fire went out. I tried again with the same result. And again. I then realised that all the largest logs were damp, so I fed in the skimpy prunings from the almond trees. They flared and crackled but burnt through in five minutes. I spent the evening with woolly tights and a hat on my head, three jumpers, thermal underwear, plus two pairs of trousers, scurrying between the kitchen to cook my meal and the stove to attend to the fire.

I had promised myself a new video once a week (the rest of the evenings I had envisaged reading or watching Greek television to improve my Greek). Hugging a rug around me, I huddled on the sofa. Virtually sitting on top of the stove, I crammed in more twigs and placed the cassette of "French and Saunders" in the video machine. I felt I needed a laugh.

I decided to sleep downstairs as it was warmer there with the stove. I didn´t even clean my teeth or change into my

pyjamas (where was the well brought up English lady now?)
I did not want to leave my cocoon, so I finally fell asleep in a
heap. It must have been about four thirty a.m. when I was
woken by a strange sound in my room. I sat bolt upright and
reached for the light switch. In the light, I saw a very large
mouse, or was it a rat? It was on the shelf where I kept my
vitamin pills, and it had knocked one container onto the floor.
I froze, terrified. The mouse/rat scampered about on the shelf
dislodging another container, this time Vitamin B, as though
it was a coconut shy. Then my Evening Primrose Oil came
hurtling down, spilling the capsules onto the floor. "That's
it", I said. The possible loss of my life enhancers which were
unavailable in Greece goaded me into action. I sprang out of
bed (well I had my socks on and I was bigger than it was),
and reached for the fly swat. I banged the wall near the shelf
and the mouse scuttled off. I retrieved my valuable pills and
jammed the lid firmly back on, then got back into bed.

I couldn't sleep. I thought "If a mouse can climb onto a shelf,
it can climb onto my bed". I lay rigid, listening to every sound
in the house; the squeaking of the window shutters sent me
into paroxysms of fear; the rustle of the branches against the
glass caused goose pimples all over.
"This is ridiculous", I mused. Here am I, alone in my house,
not even bothering to lock my door at night, yet scared witless
about a mouse. It was five-thirty a.m. and still dark, but I got
up and went into the kitchen to find the "humane mouse trap".
I could not possibly have laid the one which catches mice
and rats in its iron teeth, that would have meant I would have
to remove them, dead. The humane trap was a little cage into
which you hang a scrap of cheese onto a suspended wire.
When the mouse goes to get the cheese, the spring releases
the door, trapping the mouse inside. You are then meant to

take it and set it free, away from the house, hoping the mouse will then find another habitat.

I set the trap with a rind of cheese on the wire hook, and placed it on the shelf.

"Come on you little bugger", I said. "Here's a treat for you." After this very positive action I felt proud of myself and decided it would be safe to sleep again. I got under the covers, pulling them over my head (just in case) and fell asleep.

The next morning it was even colder. I went out onto the balcony and saw that the snow had now reached the first village on the slopes of Mud Mountain.

"Dry out more wood and cut more twigs", I said to myself.

I turned to go into the kitchen when I heard a plaintive miaow and outside, scruffy and horribly thin, was Kebab. Alive! I never thought I would be so glad to see a cat. Kebab was a character, she had a personality all of her own, I would have someone to talk to at last. I let her in, leaving the other two cats outside. Despite the cold, I knew that they could fend for themselves, as the wild cats of Greece do, and that they had a sleeping place under the house. But Kebab was fifteen years old and needed looking after. I prepared a bowl of cat food in the kitchen, she attacked it, demolishing the lot, and was then promptly sick.

"Never mind, Kebab", I said comfortingly, as I squeamishly cleared up the sick. "Take it slowly next time. Come in and get warm."

I let her into my Inner Sanctuary, the living room. She stomped over to the bed, clawed her way up, curled in a semi-circle and slept. I hadn't realised until then how much I was missing someone to talk to. I never thought a feline companion could fill that need, but it was enough, and Kebab couldn't answer me back to argue.

Because of the intense cold, I had to keep moving all day. It was warmer outside the house than in, so I cut more wood, brought large stones down from the upper road to terrace my vegetable path. I dug holes in the soil for my lemon and fig trees which Ileas had promised me. I had decided to create an English garden below the house and also needed shingle and pebbles for that. So every day I would take my Boss Bag (a brilliant invention made of plastic with four handles, to enable you to carry garden refuse), and I would go to Bottle Beach and select the same cream coloured pebbles then walk back along the goat track from the beach, relishing the sight of the silvery green olive trees, the bright yellow gorse, and just enjoying the purity of the air.

One day on my quest for pebbles, I met an old Greek lady, dressed in woollen stockings, black skirt and jumper with the uniform head scarf. She was carrying a plastic bag and a knife. "*Pou pas* (where are you going)?" she asked.
The Greeks are naturally inquisitive and always ask where are you going and why? I used to say "for a walk", but came to realise that no one on the island just went for a walk, they always had a purpose when seen on the land. I even resorted to carrying a plastic bag so that they would not think the "foreigner" was idling her day away. But this time I had a huge bag and a reason. I explained that I was off in search of pebbles and asked her where she was going.
"To collect *horta*", she replied.
"Oh dandelions", I said. "Are they good to eat now?"
"*Nai, pame mazi* (yes, come we go together)", she smiled a toothless smile and beckoned me to follow her.
We came to an olive grove off the track and to the dip in the hills where the ground was moist.
"Look", she said, "here you find the best *horta*. It must be

168

Lady with horta

young with no flowers on it, if you cut it with flowers it is too bitter to eat. You must soak it for several hours, then you can cook it, with oil and lemon." She proceeded to expertly cut the leaves and roots, then gave me a large bunch.

"This is good for your health", she said.

I thanked her profusely and went off to the beach. I compared the resourceful ways of the Greeks to those of the English. In England we would be spraying our dandelions with some deadly chemical to prevent them from spoiling our lawns. In Greece, they still believed in the beneficial power of herbs and plants.

I was once in the supermarket talking to the lady at the till. I always shopped there because the cheeses were so good. Somehow, we started talking about health (actually a favourite topic of all Greeks) and I told her that I had once had cancer. After crossing herself fervently when she heard the word and pulling down her jumper at the neck breathing "Ftot, ftoof, ftoof", down her front (this was a way of ensuring that what I had told her would never happen to her and against the "evil eye") she told me a cure.

"There is a *horta* (all greens are so named) which grows in the mountains", she said. "The gypsies pick it and then come down to the streets to sell it. But, you must know what it looks like and know when it is fresh, because there are bad (*kakos*), people who pretend they are gypsies, but they pick the *horta* in the graveyards! They try to sell it as the curative horta, but you will die if you eat that one!"

I thanked her for that advice and resolved only to buy *horta* from the greengrocers or to pick my own.

The first night of Kebab´s return I decided that she could sleep inside with me. I needed reassurance that if the mouse returned she would catch it or her scent would deter it. I again stoked the fire, then prepared a hot meal of bean soup

170

and *horta*, had an *ouzo* (only to warm me, you understand) then settled down to read with Kebab on my lap. Out of the corner of my eye, I saw a mouse scuttle from one side of the room to the other.

"Help!" I pushed Kebab to the floor, drew my feet up on the bed and shouted "Kebab, fetch it!"

Kebab ignored my plea, ignored the mouse and clawed her way back onto my lap.

"Oh God. What now?"

Here I had a useless mouse catcher, a somnolent well-fed cat who would never need to catch a mouse for food. But I could not feed her, she was only skin and bone anyway.

"Courage mon brave", I said, "You still have the trap."

I gingerly tiptoed over to where I had set the trap on the shelf, half expecting the "thing" to be in there already. I looked inside - nothing! No mouse, and to my mortification - not even any cheese!

I picked up the trap and put in yet more cheese, set it up and placed it this time on the ground where I had seen the mouse come from. Kebab slept on.

"Perhaps I didn´t set it correctly", I thought, so I delicately balanced the wire and trap door again. "I´m not sleeping down here no matter how cold it is upstairs - but I´ll leave Kebab down here."

I padded upstairs after filling my *ouzo* hot water bottle, shutting Kebab and the mouse in together. I cleaned my teeth and hastily ran a cold flannel over my face. Showering and bathing were out of the question, because of the cold. I only washed the vital parts once a day and had a bath in my hipbath after a month. That led to a cold and a cough. So I followed the Greeks´example, never get totally wet until the sun is warm. I went to sleep with my hat and tights on my head.

During the first month on my own in Trizonia I had only gone

171

to the village about twice a week, in order to get my shopping on the mainland, and for the post. I was still trying to prove that I could live alone contentedly. The post was delivered three times a week by Vlassis, a stocky middle-aged man with blue eyes. He carried the post in a large leather satchel slung on one shoulder, on the other hung a small brass horn. He would arrive, usually about eleven o'clock, go to the mini market taverna, put down his satchel on the table and blow three long blasts on the horn. This informed any of the villagers who were not already waiting, that the postman had arrived. They would all leave their houses and assemble in the taverna.

Vlassis enjoyed his job and knew everyone on the island. He would call out the names on the envelopes and hand over the appropriate mail, as if he were giving out presents to old friends. However, if the letter or card was in a foreign language, he would leave these until last. Then having dispensed with the Greek letters he would retreat to the taverna for a coffee, leaving the unclaimed and unknown post on the table outside. It was, therefore by sheer luck that I received any mail at all. The wind would whisk the paper off the table, carrying the letters to the flower beds, under chairs and even into the sea if the wind was blowing in that direction. Vlassis not only delivered mail but could deal with your electricity bill, so you didn't have to go to the mainland. He also paid out pensions to many elderly on the island. He would trot off to the housebound pensioners after the taverna, enjoying more gossip, coffees and *ouzo*s on the way.

Once in the village I would be grateful for the company, despite the fact that many of the men disapproved of my presence in the taverna whilst they were watching football. There was a big wood burning stove in there, and old Yiorgo with his lined and crinkled face always gave me a smile and

172

Postman in Trizonia

asked if I wanted any fresh eggs. Sometimes I would visit Spiros and his mother and father, Babba Yannis and Golfo, at their taverna, as they always had a huge *tzaki* roaring. They would enquire as to whether I had "*parea*" (company).

"No, I am alone", I would reply.

"We will come up and see you", they said.

But I knew they never would. They seldom went further than the village. Golfo had told me she once went to New York to visit her older son. I could not imagine how she did this journey alone. This tiny, insular Greek lady, who had never left this island in her life before. I fantasised that she had a label round her neck, with her name, address and nationality written in English. She spoke only Greek. How brave, I marvelled. Yet here she sat now, hands folded in her lap staring into the fire whilst her husband slumbered in a chair beside her. She would occasionally place another log on the fire or watch television. They didn´t need New York or even the mainland. Trizonia was the centre of their life. They worked hard for three months of the year in the summer season and were entitled to their rest in the winter.

I knew everyone on the island, or so I thought. Until one cold morning when I was walking down the lower road with my shopping trolley, for my weekly visit to the mainland, I passed two men who I had never seen before. One was around thirty, with a surly face, the other, following behind him, was an old man of about sixty. He was lean, stooped and unshaven. He wore an old sailor´s hat and his trousers were tied up with string. I noticed also that his flies were undone and his hand was clutching his penis through the trouser opening.

"Whoops!" I thought. "Who are they and what are they doing on the island?" They were not working on the marina as work had stopped and I knew all the men employed there. I decided to lock my door that night.

Next morning at nine a.m. I heard a banging on the taverna door. I staggered from my bed, dressed in my usual warm garb, went to the door to find the "Man of the Open Flies" outside. He saw me through the glass, so I couldn't retreat. I nervously slid the door open a little.

"What do you want?" I hissed.

"An *ouzo*", he said.

"Wait a minute." I shut him out, collected a glass of *ouzo* from the kitchen and handed it to him through the crack in the door.

He drank it in one gulp. Then asked: "How much?"

"Nothing", I said.

I didn't want him inside the house waiting for change. He stumped off up the path behind my house. While I quickly dressed into clean thermal underwear, I ruminated upon why he had come to the door so early. I knew the Greeks drank raki and *ouzo* to warm themselves, but what was he doing round here, eight hundred metres from the village? I decided I would go and see my English-speaking friend Xristos, to ask him if he knew this unfamiliar man. I came out of the kitchen, having washed up the dishes from the night before, to find "The Man of the Open Flies" seated in the Taverna. Thoughts of rape and violence rushed through my head as I grabbed a broom which was resting against the wall...

"What are you doing?" I yelled.

He smiled strangely. "This is a taverna, isn't it? I have come for another *ouzo*."

"Yes, well, we are closed for the winter", I said backing towards the door.

"I am working up at the Frenchman's house putting in pipes", he said. "It is very cold work. I have money for *ouzo*."

I was relieved to know why he was in this area, but not convinced of his intentions.

"Wait, I will ask my husband if I can give you one", I replied. I then rushed into the kitchen and had a conversation, in English, with my imaginary husband!

"Darling, there is a man here who wants an *ouzo*, are we allowed to sell it?"

I answered myself in the gruffest voice I could produce, and very loudly.

"Yes, okay. I´ll be out in a minute."

Thank God I hadn´t lost all my acting talent and voice projection from my RADA training. I took a three-quarter full bottle of *ouzo* from the kitchen shelf and swept into the taverna.

"Here you are - my husband says you can have this." I thrust it into his hands. His eyes brightened at the sight of the bottle. "How much?" he asked.

"Oh nothing", I said in desperation. "But that is the last bottle we have." I wanted him to leave. His flies were still gaping open.

"You husband is a kind man", he said as I pushed him out of the door. "Is he Greek?"

"Yes, of course!" I replied.

It was only after I shut and locked the door on him I realised my conversation to my "husband" had been in English! So he couldn´t have understood a word of it anyway.

Next day when I went to the village for the post I saw Xristos. I told him about the strange man and the bottle of *ouzo*.

"*Leez*", he laughed, "that man is the local drunk from the mainland. Yesterday he come to the village in the afternoon and he could not walk straight. No one gives him a drink here on this island. We did not understand how he got like that if he was working." Xristos then proceeded to tell everyone in the taverna of my mistake. They laughed and offered to buy me an *ouzo*.

A week later, when I was driving down the road on the mainland towards the baker's shop, I came round a bend and had to brake violently because there, in a hole in the road, with just his head sticking out, was "The Man of the Open Flies!" There were no "Go Slow" or "Men Working" signs anywhere near him. He could have been decapitated. He slowly raised his head, then brought out a pickaxe which he waved at me, grinning stupidly. Maybe he didn't survive the road digging job - as I haven't seen him since that day.

I had been in Trizonia for nearly two months when suddenly one morning, Spring arrived. Aspassia told me Spring always arrived on the twenty-eighth of February. The snow had melted on Mud Mountain and the air was warm. I stood on the balcony without the need for my hat or thermal underwear. From then on I took my breakfast outside. I gazed at the transformation. The almond trees were budding, cherry trees too, there were tiny yellow star-shaped flowers in the crevices in my garden, and crocuses and miniature harebells were pushing through the soil to say "hello."

I now had no need to work physically hard all day in order to get my circulation going. I sat outside in the sun all morning, meditating, reading and studying Greek. One morning Ileas arrived on Panagia bringing me two lemon trees and a fig tree.

"Now it is warmer we can plant these", he said.

He buried the roots deeply, firming them in with his boots, put a stout stick beside each trunk and tied the tree to them with a bit of sacking.

"You must find some humus now for the trees and your garden, *Leez*, before it gets too warm."

Then Aspassia toiled up the steep path, stopping at every bend. After coffee and advice from them both as to which seeds I should now be planting in my newly created vegetable patch, we set off together to find the humus.

Aspassia told me to look under bushes and trees which did not face the sun. With my shovel I dug up the sweet-smelling rotted leaves and learnt to find the best patches of humus from all round the island. Every day now I set myself this satisfying job. If I wanted to be self-sufficient, my vegetables needed nurturing.

One day while on this errand, I had walked across a meadow, blue carpeted with harebells, under some olive trees, and I came across a large grey stone, which was worn into the shape of a seat. I sat on it. The view was incredible. It faced southwest and the afternoon sun had warmed the stone. From this point I could see the valley where the spring water collected near the old well through groves of silvery olive trees, to the hills on the far side of the island, and the track between them leading to Red Beach. Across the sea was a high range of mountains, still snow-capped, and to the right I could make out the finger of land which protected Lepanto Harbour. There was no sound, apart from the occasional cry of a bird or the braying of a donkey and the tinkle of goats' bells. Such unpolluted natural beauty was a privilege to behold.

In the winter and early spring the sun disappeared from the balcony of my house at two p.m. so I decided to do all my jobs in the garden and house in the morning, then to take myself off to the sunny stone seat after lunch each day. I would then be able to brown my weather-beaten face and to meditate and read in peace. The cats were still a distraction, fighting amongst themselves or crying for food. It was a relief to get away from them. So this became my schedule, as I needed to set myself goals or I would have become very slothful. I painted the water tanks, pipes, path lights, outside; decorated the Taverna, painted the ceiling where the rain had come through in the autumn and continued to tend the garden, now only dressed in shorts and a T-shirt. Life was wonderful!

One warm day in the middle of February I was sitting on my stone seat reading, in total tranquillity. Suddenly there was a gunshot and a bullet whizzed past my ear, hit a large stone behind me and ricocheted off it.

"Christ!" I breathed. "What's going on?" I picked up my book and fled to the half built Frenchman's house for shelter. I peered around the pillar and saw in the valley two men with guns.

Bang! Crack!

Another gun shot with the bullet landing close to my shelter. I crouched low on the terrace and watched the men. I wasn't going to stand up and wave. That would have made it too easy for them. I became paranoid, imagining they were shooting at me because I was an English "foreigner" and they resented my presence on the island.

I waited about fifteen minutes, trying to think of the Greek words for "gun" and "shoot". If I had known the words I would have accosted them as they walked back and asked them why they were shooting at me. Frustrated and fearful, I crept back to my house. Home again. I poured myself a large Metaxa then leafed through the dictionary to find the words. Dictionary in hand, I waited for half an hour, but there was no sign of the terrorists, nor any more gun shots. That night I locked my doors and put my blunted axe under my pillow.

I was woken from a deep sleep next morning by a gun shot right near the house, then another and another. "So, it's siege time now!"

I tore round the house blocking the windows with bits of wood, then locked myself in the cold room, which had no windows I remained in there for about an hour, but realised that I would freeze to death if I stayed any longer. I tiptoed out cautiously, blunt axe in my hand, and looked over the balcony to the path below. There were the two men, in camouflage gear, guns slung over their shoulders, ambling along towards my house.

"Eh. You two. Why are you shooting at me?" I hollered from the balcony, fear giving way to anger.

They paused and looked up. I ducked below the table.

"What did you say, Madam?" one said politely.

"You heard me. You shot at me in my house today, and yesterday when I was sitting in the field."

They shook their heads and laughed. "*Oxi, Madam. Lathos einai!* (That is a mistake) We are here to shoot birds. The season has started." Whereupon they held up their kill - two magpies and a pathetic sparrow, heads dangling.

"Well, don´t shoot so near my house again", I commanded. I retreated to my inner sanctuary, knees still shaking. "What an idiot I was!" I had forgotten that the Greeks will shoot birds. Not just for sport, but to eat. It must be a residual from the war when they were forced to eat any living animal or bird, or starve. Everyone had guns in Greece and sometimes no licence. They still lived in fear of being occupied by the Turks, or Italians, or English again, and after the Hellenic history I couldn´t blame their trigger-happy obsession. I just did not want to be target practice.

February passed into March and with the new month came many changes in Trizonia. Doors of houses were opened all day again. Houses and boats were freshly painted. Mattresses, blankets and washing were taken outside. The villagers would sit outside in the sun, smiling and drinking coffee. The fishing boats circled the bay at night with their large lamps, looking for octopus and I would hear the slap, slap on the stones as they tenderised their catch in the morning. The sheep were brought over from the mainland in small *caiques*, bleating all the way across and would graze on the island which was still green. Easter was approaching and the lambs and kids needed fattening for their inevitable fate on a spit. The almond trees were in full bloom, flowers struggled through the soil; red poppies appeared in profusion, camomile and daisies raised their face to the sun. Spring was definitely here!

With the new season came a realisation for me that I had been in Greece, on a tiny island - a *"xeni"*- alone for over two months and I had survived. I had battled with the weather conditions (I still needed a fire at night), my Greek had improved, I had learnt a lot about self-sufficiency, how to find wild *horta* and asparagus. Liberally dosed with humus, my garden was now producing spinach, lettuce and beans, during the summer I would be self-sufficient with vegetable and fruit. The Taverna was looking clean and I would be opening to yacht owners soon. There would be company again, voices, laughter, talk of where they´d sailed from and where they were making for. From now on I could expect a flow of visitors and friends passing through.

But was it enough? I felt proud of my achievements of the past eighteen months. I´d certainly changed my life, but lately I found a doubt creeping into my thoughts. Was it enough to pass the day in idle chatter with my Greek friends, to swim and soak up the sun? Was it enough to play the role of confidant to ever-changing crews of passing yachts or to live a kind of extended summer holiday. No, I needed a "raison d´être"..., I knew that if my life here was to really work, I must have a purpose. But what could I do?

I walked to the village in time for the arrival of the post. I would catch my letters before they blew away this time. Vlassis arrived, blew his horn and read out the names. He handed out all but two. He fingered them, peering closely back and front then handed them to me, saying "*Leez Parkerre*." One was from the Inland Revenue and had been re-addressed from my son's house, the other in unmistakable scrawl was from Martina. I asked Xristos for a coffee and sat under the mulberry tree to read the letter. Inside the envelope was only a postcard with a picture of "Houses in Wimbledon", Martina with her pen had added rain and black clouds.

It read: "Weather here predictable for the time of year! Can't wait to hear about your winter. I shall be arriving on eleventh of March. OK? Will arrive usual time unless you say no, Mart."

It was dated second of February.

"What date is it Xristos?" I asked.

"Today, *Leez*, it is Friday the eleventh of March."

CHAPTER 14

FINALE

There is no better way for me to formulate ideas and to clarify my mind than talking to a friend. When Martina arrived at the village I realised how much I had missed her and the reciprocity which can only be found with a soulmate, and someone who speaks the same language. All the pent up emotions, doubts and fears which I had contained over the last three months came tumbling out as we sat together in the Taverna.

"So Liz, if you have doubts about running a taverna for the rest of time and know that you cannot be happy doing only this work, what other ways have you thought about so you can go on living here, presuming you still want to?"

"Yes, I want to be here in Greece, and I´m not such a defeatist that I would give up the yacht club after one year. Alison can run that, but I want to feed peoples´ minds not just their bodies. I´m still searching for my own answers in a metaphysical sense. The hospital told me in November that I was free of cancer and that I only needed to return once a ·year for a check up, and I believe I am cured, so I can live here. Do you know I am fifty-five years old and it has taken me all these years to realise a dream - and now I have fulfilled it I am looking for something more! How contrary I am, I suppose that´s a Libran trait?"

"Dreams change too Lizzie. You know if you have a recurrent dream and then, in reality, you achieve that dream, you stop having it!"

"M´mm - that´s so - Maybe I should travel now to India and find my roots where I was born, or I could start a Healing Centre here in Greece, or perhaps...?"

Libran Characteristics are:
Indecisiveness; a need for harmony and balance; and a desire to help others...

THE END FOR NOW

Further publications by Melina:

Cyprus - Byzantine Churches and Monasteries
Byzantine frescoes and mosaics in 39 churches and monasteries with a comprehensive historical introduction.
By Ewald Hein, Andrija Jakovljevic, Brigitte Kleidt
Hardcover, Book Jacket, 198 p., 190 col. pict., 19x 24 cm, 1996
79,00 DM
German, ISBN 3-929255-21-9
English, ISBN 3-929255-15-4

Tibet - Der Weiße Tempel von Tholing
(The White Temple of Tholing)
400 years old temple paintings in the west of Tibet with a foreword of Dalai Lama. Comprehensive historical view of Buddhistic development in Tibet.
By Ewald Hein and Günther Boelmann
Hardcover, Book Jacket, 188 p., 52 col. pict., 19 x 24 cm, 1994
79,00 DM, German, ISBN 3-929255-06-5

Ethiopia - Christian Africa
Art, Churches and Culture
In the fissured and in some regions hardly accessible highlands of Ethiopia there are still places of a living Christianity which is older than the Christian churches of Europe. Evidence of old tradition can be found in Axum, the ancient capital of Abyssinia, where they say the Ark of the Covenant is preserved until today. The illustrated book shows the excellent painted churches in this Christian part of Africa.
By Ewald Hein and Brigitte Kleidt
Hardcover, Book Jacket, abt. 210 p., with 200 col. pict., 29 x 24 cm
79,00 DM
English ISBN 3-929255-28-6
German ISBN 3-929255-27-8
Date of publication end 1998